Kate and the Revolution

Books by John Rowe Townsend

THE CREATURES

FOREST OF THE NIGHT

GOOD NIGHT, PROF, DEAR

GOOD-BYE TO THE JUNGLE

THE INTRUDER

THE ISLANDERS

NOAH'S CASTLE

PIRATE'S ISLAND

THE SUMMER PEOPLE

TOP OF THE WORLD

TROUBLE IN THE JUNGLE

(originally GUMBLE'S YARD)

THE VISITORS

MODERN POETRY

A SOUNDING OF STORYTELLERS

WRITTEN FOR CHILDREN

John Rowe Townsend

◄I( )I►

Kate and the Revolution

◄I( )I►

J. B. Lippincott · New York

AUTHOR'S NOTE

This story has no message and no hidden meanings
that I am aware of. Please don't take it too seriously.
It is for fun. J.R.T.

Kate and the Revolution
First published in Great Britain under the title
A Foreign Affair by Kestrel Books, Penguin Books Ltd.
Copyright © 1982 by John Rowe Townsend
Printed in
the United States of America. For information address
J. B. Lippincott Junior Books, 10 East 53rd Street,
New York, N.Y. 10022. Published simultaneously in
Canada by Fitzhenry & Whiteside Limited, Toronto.

10 9 8 7 6 5 4 3 2 1

First American Edition

Library of Congress Cataloging in Publication Data
Townsend, John Rowe.
  Kate and the revolution.

  British ed. published in 1982 under title: A foreign
affair.
  Summary: Seventeen-year-old Kate falls in love with
a prince and finds herself in the middle of a revolu-
tion.
  I. Title.
PZ7.T6637Kat 1983   [Fic]   81-48605
ISBN 0-397-32015-9
ISBN 0-397-32016-7 (lib. bdg.)

To his Imperial Majesty, Maximilian Franz Josef,
King and Emperor,
otherwise known as Richard Beck,
with happy memories of hours in school
wasted (perhaps) on make-believe

1

⟡⟨ ⟩⟡

Kate Milbank's quarrel with her father, Edward, had been going on all week. Until the day of Susan Baker's party it was conducted by correspondence. This was because, five days a week, Kate and Edward didn't see each other. Edward was a journalist and worked at night. He was at home in the daytime when Kate was at school, and left for his office before she got home. When he and Kate had things to say to each other, they left notes.

Kate and Edward quarreled about once a month, on average. It was usually over something trivial. They loved each other dearly, but often found each other irritating. Kate complained that Edward was vague and forgetful. Edward complained that Kate was bossy.

Edward, who was tall and thin and had wavy silver-gray hair, was Foreign Editor of a London newspaper, the *Daily Intelligence*. His wife had left him three years earlier, when Kate was not quite fourteen. Since then, Kate had gradually taken charge of the household. Edward's job involved a lot of decision making on such questions as whether to spend large amounts of the paper's money to send reporters on overseas assignments, and whether to print reports that might lead to diplomatic crises. When he got home, the last thing Edward wanted to do was to make decisions. So Kate made them instead. She did the shopping and organized the repairs and replacements. If a room needed decorating, Kate decorated it, and Edward didn't even notice that it had been done.

The quarrel that week began in a low key. On Monday night Kate left a note for Edward, asking, "*Must* you leave dirty saucepans around and crumbs on the carpet?" On Tuesday morning she found a reply scrawled at the foot of her note, saying "In yesterday's circumstances, yes." On Tuesday night, Kate inquired, "*What* circumstances?" On Wednesday morning, the note was still there, with no further comment from Edward. Apparently he hadn't seen it.

On Wednesday afternoon Kate had a tiresome interview at school about the subjects she was to do the next year; then she had to go and buy some cleaning materials for the house. When she got home, she was hot and cross and just in the mood to be irritated all over again. So underneath the words "*What* circumstances?" that she'd written the previous night, she added a row of five question marks, each bigger than the last, followed by an enormous exclamation mark; then she put the note where Edward couldn't fail to find it, under the coffeepot.

On Thursday morning she found that Edward had added the word "Crisis" to the note. On Thursday night she wrote crossly beneath this, "*What* crisis?" On Friday morning, the note still lay on the kitchen table, with the further message "Can't remember now. Too much water under bridge." On Friday night, Kate filled the remaining space on the scrap of paper, which by now was a bit grubby and smeared with jelly, with the words "Oh, you are *hopeless!*" And on Saturday afternoon, when at last they were at home together, Kate and Edward had a row.

Like all such rows, this one generated more heat than light. Old grievances were brought out and old accusations thrown around. Kate claimed that she worked her fingers to the bone for an unhelpful and unappreciative father. Edward claimed that he risked heart failure or nervous breakdown in a grueling job to support a nagging and bad-tempered child. And so on. In the end, Kate declared that she was longing for the day when she could leave home, and Edward proclaimed that it couldn't come soon enough for him. Both statements were untrue, but that didn't prevent them from hurting.

At about teatime the battle ended, both sides having run out of ammunition. But neither of them was ready to make peace. And in midevening Kate announced that she would go to Susan Baker's party after all.

Edward asked, "Who's Susan Baker?"

"At a modest estimate," Kate said, "I have mentioned Susan Baker one hundred and seventy-seven times this year so far. It just shows how much you listen to me. Susan Baker is an awful girl in my class at school." She added bitterly, "I expect it will be an awful party."

"If she's an awful girl and you expect it to be an awful party," Edward said, "why go?"

There are some conversations that can be likened to tennis matches, in that the aim of each participant is to score points off the other. Applying this comparison, it could be said that Edward had now lobbed up a weak return and given Kate the opening for a forehand smash. She took it.

"*Anything*," she declared, "would be better than spending the evening in this godforsaken house with you!" And she flounced out with an air of having won game, set, and match.

It was a hollow victory. The weather was wet and windy, and Kate had to battle her way for half a mile on foot to Susan Baker's house. And the party was every bit as bad as she'd feared. Susan's parents, instead of considerately going out for the evening, lurked in the background, worrying over the possibility of broken glasses and stains on the carpet. The drink was the kind of sweet fizzy stuff that Kate particularly disliked. She didn't think much of Susan's music, either. And there wasn't enough room to dance, but people were trying to do so anyway, and treading on everybody's feet. After half an hour Kate had had enough, and was also beginning to feel remorseful about the things she'd said to Edward. She was on the point of slipping quietly away home.

It was Cecily Higgins who prevented Kate from leaving. Cecily buttonholed Kate on her way to the bathroom and asked her to come and meet Rudi. Cecily's father was a senior civil servant, and he sometimes entertained important people from abroad. It appeared that Rudi was one of these, and that as he was nearer to Cecily's age than to her father's, she'd brought him along to Susan Baker's party. Cecily took Kate across to meet him.

He was sitting in a corner of the room, surrounded by girls. He wore a well-cut and obviously expensive suit. He was dark and very handsome. And his first words to Kate were among the most surprising she'd heard in her life.

He said, "Hello, beautiful!"

2

Kate didn't expect compliments from good-looking young men. She wasn't under any illusions about her appearance. The truth is that she was dumpy. She was a little below average height and a little above average width. It wasn't her fault. She didn't nibble between meals or eat a lot of candy. It was all in her genes— her genes from her mother's side. Edward ate twice as much as Kate did and was as thin as a rail. As she often pointed out, it was grossly unfair.

Kate's face was as round as the rest of her. Her hair was an ordinary brown. True, she had nice dark eyes and a good complexion. But beautiful? Oh, no. She was under no illusions about that.

There was no doubt that Rudi was good-looking. Ravishing, in fact. He was probably in his early twenties. He had a thin oval face, dark hair with a slight, crisp wave in it, and dark straight brows. His eyes were brown, his skin olive but not swarthy. He spoke excellent English with a faint, intriguing foreign accent.

And he had said, "Hello, beautiful." Kate couldn't quite believe she'd heard him correctly.

"Do you mean me?" she asked.

Rudi flashed a stunning smile at her. "Of course," he said. "Who else?"

"Well . . ." Kate, a little bemused, indicated those around her. Rudi dismissed them with a shrug of his shoulders.

"I have been watching you for twenty minutes," he told her. "And I said to myself, 'There is the girl I want to meet.' "

A girl called Deirdre Thomas who had been sitting next to Rudi rose to her feet.

"Seems to me you two should be getting acquainted," she said sourly, and she left. Rudi patted the vacant space and Kate sat down beside him.

"Do you have a boyfriend?" Rudi asked her.

"As a matter of fact," said Kate, "I haven't. Not just now. I have had before and I daresay I will have again. At the moment the post is vacant. But I don't know why that should interest you."

"I am astonished," said Rudi. "I should have thought you would have a dozen at least."

Kate was flattered. A wild hope sprang up in a corner of her mind that perhaps after all she *was* the kind of girl that young men like Rudi found attractive. But she beat it down instantly.

"Listen," she said. "I'm quite intelligent. I get A's in most subjects. But you couldn't know that from looking at me across a room. In appearance I only get B minus. Or maybe C. Some would say F. So what are you getting at?"

Rudi flashed the smile. "The English," he said, "have

a strange taste in women. They like them tall and skinny. Latins like them fat. But in my country we like them . . ." He looked her up and down appreciatively. "We like them just right."

Kate said coldly, "How would you like it if I said that according to my taste in men you were 'just right'?"

"I should like it very much," said Rudi. He smiled for the third time. The smile did have a curiously melting effect. Against her will Kate found herself half smiling in return.

"Don't trust him, Kate," said Deirdre Thomas, coming back.

"Anyway, who's 'we'?" Kate demanded of Rudi. "Which *is* your country?"

"A country you've never heard of," said Rudi.

"Tell me," said Kate. "And I bet I *have* heard of it."

A new tape started up. It was particularly noisy, and drowned Rudi's reply. Then somebody at his other side drew him into conversation. Kate was left momentarily to her own thoughts. Her attention was caught by a man, several years older than the other guests, who was standing on his own beside a window. He was blond, with close-cropped hair and a pale, expressionless face. His shoulders were broad, and he looked decidedly tough.

Deirdre Thomas had followed Kate's eyes. "That's Rudi's interpreter," she remarked. "The funny thing is, he doesn't seem to know much English."

"Whereas Rudi knows plenty," said Kate. "Odd."

"Very odd."

10

"Well," said Kate a minute later, "I was asked to meet him, and I've met him. I think I'll go now."

She started to get up. Rudi hadn't been looking at her, but his hand went out and took hers. He stopped talking to the other person and turned to Kate.

"Stay where you are, darling," he said.

"I'm not your darling!" said Kate.

"That's a pity," said Rudi.

Cecily Higgins came up. "You wouldn't have heard the doorbell," she said to Rudi, "but my father arrived just now. He's come to fetch you. He wants to take you to the Courtenays'. You remember?"

"I remember," Rudi said. "A tragedy. The party has just become interesting. Now, where is my hostess?"

"Susan?" said Cecily. "Oh, she's around somewhere. I wouldn't bother in all this crush. I'll say good-bye for you, Rudi. I'll tell her you had a lovely time, okay?"

"Okay," said Rudi. He rolled the syllables round his tongue. "Okay. You are very tactful, Cecily. Good-bye, Kate. I shall see you again, shall I not?"

"I doubt it," said Kate.

"What is your telephone number?"

Kate didn't answer.

"Oh, well, I expect it's in the book," Rudi said. He allowed himself to be led away. The tough-looking blond man detached himself from the wall and followed him, a few feet behind. Kate stayed where she was, meditating. In a minute or two Cecily Higgins reappeared.

"Well, he got to know you," she said. "I think that's what he came for, really."

11

Kate was startled. "You mean, he wanted to know me before he'd even seen me?"

"Yes."

"But why? Why should he want to know *me*? How did he know I even exist?"

"I think my dad mentioned your dad, and I said I knew you."

"Did you say I was a glamor girl or something?"

"Frankly, Kate, no. But he does seem to fancy you, doesn't he?"

"How long is he here for? And where *does* he come from, anyway?"

"He's only here for a week or two, on a visit. He comes from Essenheim."

"Where's Essenheim? In Germany?"

"No. It's an independent country."

"He said I wouldn't have heard of it," Kate said. "And he was right. I haven't."

"Neither had I until a few days ago. It's a tiny place in the middle of Europe. That's all I know about it. If you want to know any more, you'll have to ask Rudi."

"You seem to think I'm going to see him again."

"I'm sure you are," said Cecily.

"I still don't understand," said Kate. And then, after a pause: "So Rudi comes from Essenheim. What does he *do* there?"

"He's the Crown Prince," said Cecily.

3

————— ❖❲ ❳❖ —————

When Kate got home, she and Edward fell into each other's arms and swore undying affection. This was usual. Their rows all led eventually to a lovely hug-and-make-up session.

Edward explained that the crisis that had led to the unwashed saucepans was a sudden recall to his office over an international incident that had now blown over. He apologized for the mess and for pretending to forget the reason. Kate apologized for putting saucepans ahead of international affairs. Both of them blamed themselves with all the energy they had previously devoted to blaming each other. Then they sat down at the kitchen table to drink coffee and swap the week's gossip of school and office. After a while Kate said to Edward, "What do you know about Essenheim?"

Edward said, "As much as anybody does. Which isn't much."

Kate asked, "Why isn't it much?"

Edward said, "Nobody goes there and nothing happens. I can't remember when we last had a story from

13

Essenheim. There isn't even a wire-service reporter there. It's just a backwater."

Kate said, "That can't be *all* you know. Tell me more. To begin with, where exactly *is* Essenheim?"

Edward said, "You know where Switzerland is. And beyond Switzerland is Serenia, right? Serenia's like another Switzerland, but more so. Rich and comfortable. No inflation, no crime, no unemployment. No drunkenness, no immorality. No fun. Well, Essenheim's at the far side of Serenia. It's a bit of the old Austrian Empire that got forgotten in the peace treaty after World War I. Just a few thousand people, mostly peasant farmers, but they make good wine there, or so I'm told."

"I like the sound of it," said Kate. "Could we go there on a package tour?"

Edward said, "You're joking. There aren't any package tours to Essenheim. It's ruled by an old fellow they call the Prince Laureate, who doesn't like anything as modern as tourism. His family were princes of Essenheim under the Austrian Emperor. There isn't an Emperor anymore, but Essenheim still trundles on as if World War I had never happened. Now, why the sudden interest?"

"I've just met somebody from there," said Kate.

Edward sat up straight. A newspaperman always pricks up his ears when he hears something that sounds as if it might lead to a story. "Who is he?" he asked. "What's he doing in London?"

"You don't know that it's a he," said Kate. "It might be a she. Why is it always assumed that a person of unstated sex is masculine?"

14

"I know it's a he," said Edward. "I can tell by the look in your eye."

"All right, it is a he," Kate admitted. "And what he is, is the Crown Prince."

Edward pondered this for a moment. Then he asked, "Who says?"

"Cecily Higgins says. He's staying at their house. And her father came to collect him from Susan's party."

"Hmmm," said Edward. "It sounds as if he's the genuine article. James Higgins wouldn't be entertaining a phony. Now, let's see if my memory can supply me with your man's name. Prince Rudolf, is that it?"

"That's right," said Kate. "Rudi. And by the way, he said he wanted to see me again."

"Does he know your address or telephone number?"

"I didn't give them to him. I wasn't sure I liked him. But he can easily find out."

"Why were you not sure you liked him?" Edward asked.

"He was trying to pick me up. Calling me 'darling' and 'beautiful.'"

"That sounds interesting."

"It sounds ridiculous!" Kate said. "I mean, you only have to look at me to see how ridiculous it is. The Crown Prince of wherever-it-is making advances to the plump, plain daughter of a London journalist!"

"You're not plain at all," said Edward loyally. "Or plump either, really. Just pleasantly rounded."

"Come off it," said Kate. "You may deceive yourself, but you can't deceive *me*. It's Rudi who's beautiful. I'm not."

15

"As to that," Edward said, "we'd better agree to differ. But anyway, if he does show up, I'd be quite glad to meet him. Why not ask him here for a meal? Unless of course you really don't want to see him again."

"Oh, I expect I could stand it," said Kate.

Actually, she realized as she spoke that her interest in Rudi was increasing rapidly. She wondered if she'd been too ready to fend him off. After all, he *was* a Crown Prince, and the most handsome young man she'd ever met, and the only one who'd said such complimentary things to her. . . .

She lay awake that night thinking about him.

The next morning, Sunday, she was still thinking about him. And by now she knew she hoped very much that he'd meant it when he'd spoken of seeing her again. She was on tenterhooks all day. The doorbell rang twice and the telephone four times, and each time her heart pounded, but each time it turned out not to be Rudi. There was no sign of life from him on any of the next three days, either. On the fourth day, Thursday, Kate brought herself to telephone Cecily Higgins and inquire. But Rudi had only been with the Higginses for the weekend. Cecily knew nothing about his later movements.

On Friday Kate was in a sensible mood and told herself that the incident was of no importance, that nothing was going to come of it, and that she might as well put Rudi out of her mind and get on with her life. Then on Saturday he telephoned.

Kate was out shopping, and Edward answered the phone. By the time Kate came back, Edward had invited Rudi to come round as soon as he could, and had asked him to lunch.

Kate found that her heart was pounding again. But all she said was "What are we going to give him?"

"Oh, you can go out and get some Chinese or Indian food," Edward said.

"That doesn't sound very princely."

"He's only a *minor* prince," said Edward. "And anyway, a princely stomach is much the same as any other."

"He might not *like* Chinese or Indian."

"He does. I asked him."

"You always know the right question to ask, don't you?" said Kate.

She just happened to be looking out the sitting-room window half an hour later when Rudi arrived. He was in a big old-fashioned Rolls-Royce, which drew up impressively in the Milbanks' drive.

And Rudi wasn't alone. There was a man in a peaked cap sitting beside him, looking like a displaced chauffeur, which presumably he was, because Rudi was at the wheel. And there was another man sitting in the back, half lost amid the upholstery and giving the impression of trying to look as if he wasn't there at all. Kate couldn't be sure, but he looked rather like the man who'd been with Rudi at Susan Baker's party.

Kate answered the doorbell with Edward standing just behind her. Rudi was on the doorstep; the other two men had stayed in the car. In contrast to the expensive suit he'd been wearing at Susan's party, Rudi's apparel now consisted of jeans and a duffel coat, and

17

he looked rather like a student. Inappropriately, though, he was carrying a large and showy bunch of flowers.

Rudi thrust the flowers into Kate's arms and then kissed her emphatically on both cheeks. And while she was still dazed, he pressed forward so that she had to step back, and in a moment he was inside the house.

Once the door was closed behind him, Rudi seemed to relax. In a cheerful, friendly tone, he said, "Hello, Kate. Thank you for letting me come."

"It wasn't me, really," Kate pointed out. "It was my father. Here he is. Dad, this is . . ." She paused, then appealed to Rudi. "How do I describe you?"

"Just Rudi." And, turning to Edward and putting out his hand, "How do you do, sir? I'm pleased to make your acquaintance. I know quite a lot about you."

"Somehow I thought you probably did," said Edward.

4

The next twenty minutes seemed slightly unreal to Kate. In the sitting room of the Milbanks' Victorian semidetached house, Rudi sat at ease and chatted to her father, while she was very conscious that outside in the driveway two men sat in the car waiting for him. After the display with flowers and kisses on the doorstep, Rudi hadn't paid any special attention to Kate. He and Edward made small talk about weather and Essenheim wines and their respective European travels. Kate had the impression that they were circling round each other, not yet ready to come to grips.

Rudi hadn't mentioned the two men outside. When, in a lull in the conversation, Kate offered to make coffee, she asked Rudi if she should take some to his companions.

"Oh, *those!*" said Rudi. "No, Kate, you need do nothing for them. It is by no wish of mine that they are here. I would have come by myself and greatly preferred it. It was the Essenheim Consul in London who provided me with a chauffeur and an interpreter. I have no need of either, but I've had the doubtful pleasure of their company all week. They are, as you say in English, keeping an eye on me."

"Oh," said Kate. She went to the kitchen and loaded the coffeepot. When she returned to the sitting room with a tray, the talk between Edward and Rudi had taken a more interesting turn.

"You see," Rudi was saying, "nothing can happen in Essenheim while my uncle—he is actually my great-uncle—remains Prince Laureate. He will retain Dr. Stockhausen as Prime Minister; he can't imagine doing anything else. Dr. Stockhausen has been in charge for thirty years. He is very rigid in his views. And while this state of affairs lasts, we shall continue in isolation, with no democracy, no new science or technology, no tourism, no industry, and no increased production or exports of our excellent wine. We shall vegetate."

"There are some in other countries who would envy you for that," Edward remarked mildly.

"It doesn't seem enviable to *me!*" Rudi said with some vigor. "And the wealth and power stay in the same hands forever. There's an aristocracy, a small professional class, and one very rich man—Herr Finkel—who owns almost everything in sight. The rest are shopkeepers and peasants."

"Presumably you're part of the aristocracy yourself," Edward observed.

"Yes, indeed. But that is no great privilege. It's a very small aristocracy and very—what's your word?—stuffy."

"You're pretty frank about it," Edward said. "After

all, you only met me half an hour ago. Does the Prince Laureate know how you feel?"

"Oh, yes, Uncle Ferdy knows, but he's not too worried. He still thinks I'll grow out of it. He's not a bad old boy in his way."

"Yet he has you watched?"

"Dr. Stockhausen has me watched. He and Uncle Ferdy put their heads together and decided to send me on a kind of Grand Tour, visiting the royal friends and relations. Descendants of deposed monarchs, most of them. The Prince hopes I'll return to Essenheim reconciled to my lot. Well, I'm almost at the end of the tour. I go home next month."

"And are you reconciled?" Edward asked.

"No."

"What is it you want, Rudi?" Kate inquired.

"I want a free, modern Essenheim."

"It's easy to say you want your country free and modern," Edward pointed out. "Everybody says that everywhere. What do you plan to *do* about it?"

"Well . . ." Rudi began. He hesitated, then went on. "I will, if I may, speak to you off the record. I am, as you know, the Crown Prince. But that gives me very little influence while my uncle retains the throne and Dr. Stockhausen retains my uncle's confidence. Moreover, Dr. Stockhausen would like to replace me as heir with my cousin Friedrich, who is a weak personality and would do as he was told. Now, if *I* were Prince Laureate, things would be different."

"So you want to depose your uncle?" Edward asked.

"I don't *want* to depose my uncle. I love and respect

him. But I think it is in the interest of Essenheim for him to cease to be Prince Laureate. That is the only way we can enter a new era."

"Can't people vote for a different government?" Kate asked.

"We don't have elections in Essenheim. My uncle is an absolute ruler. He thinks elections have been the ruin of Europe. If it hadn't been for elections, he says, the old Kings and Emperors would still be on their thrones and the world would be a better place."

"Doubtful," Edward remarked. "However, in circumstances such as you describe, an army coup is what usually happens."

"That is true. But in Essenheim the army, which is very small, is led by a certain Colonel Schweiner, who was merely a sergeant until my uncle promoted him. He has a dominating personality but not much intelligence. In my opinion he is too stupid to lead a revolution. Fortunately, there are some who think that I myself am qualified to head a movement to bring Essenheim into the twentieth century."

"You mean *you* want to lead a coup?" asked Kate.

"Not unless all else fails. If I could persuade my uncle that it was time for him to step down in my favor, the way would be open for peaceful change."

"And what are you asking *me* to do?" said Edward.

"I suggest that you print an article on the unrest in Essenheim and the dissatisfaction with the reactionary old regime."

"Maybe I will," said Edward, "when I'm convinced of it."

"I can give you a great deal more information," Rudi said. "But you must agree that it will not be attributed to me. And I must ask you not to print it for a few weeks. If it appeared now, my uncle and Dr. Stockhausen might well guess that I was the source."

"How will a story in the *Daily Intelligence* help your cause?" Edward asked. "People overestimate the effect of newspaper articles. I don't suppose for a moment that one story in a British paper would demoralize the old regime or bring you to power."

"No. But it would win the support of your liberal-minded readership. Soon after it appeared, you would receive a letter from an exiled Essenheimer in London, a Dr. Falkstadt, appealing for support for a 'Free Essenheim' campaign. I trust you would print it. And, the generosity and liberal principles of your readers being well known—"

"You think they'd rally round," said Edward. He thought for a moment. "Well, they might. *Daily Intelligence* readers yearn for worthy causes to support, and the more distant the better. We haven't had a suitable one for quite a while. Yes, Rudi, you've interested me. And now let's have some detail to back up your general assertions."

Kate said crossly, "You won't be needing me. I'll go out for that Chinese food. Then Rudi can regale you with further fascinating information over the sweet-and-sour. I'll have mine in my room and get on with some homework."

She could have wept with humiliation and disappointment. It seemed clear that Rudi was interested in the *Daily Intelligence*, not in her. He'd only wanted to get to know her so he could talk to Edward. Now that she'd played her part she was of no further interest, or so it appeared. Beautiful, indeed! Darling, indeed! As for the flowers, she had a good mind to pitch them into the trash.

But now Rudi surprised her. "Perhaps you'll let me come with you, Kate," he said. "I should love to go for a short walk. No doubt your father can be preparing the further questions he will wish to ask me."

Kate looked inquiringly at Edward.

"No doubt I can," he agreed dryly. "Try not to be too long."

The big old Rolls-Royce was still in the drive. The chauffeur had moved to the driver's seat. He was now reading a popular newspaper, folded back to display the picture of a nearly naked pinup girl.

The other man was standing in the driveway ahead of them. Seen at close range, his pale face was rubbery and thick lipped, and his nose slightly squashed. He looked like the sort of man you wouldn't care to pick a quarrel with. He spoke to Rudi in a language unknown to Kate, full of plosives and gutturals.

"Speak English, not Essenheimisch, please," Rudi told him, and went on, "This is Miss Milbank. She is a very special young lady. I am taking her for a walk."

The man's face cracked into a kind of grin, which sat on him like lipstick on a gorilla.

"Good day, gracious young lady," he said, and stood aside.

"Karl is an Essenheimer," Rudi told her. "In Essenheim, all ladies are young and gracious, and all gentle-men are gallant. It's our standard form of address."

He put an arm round her waist as they turned out of the drive. "No, don't push it away," he whispered. "I'll explain to you in a minute."

"I think you'd better," Kate said when they were out in the street. "You make passes at me in public, and then in private you don't show any interest. Just what are you up to?"

"Kate," said Rudi, "please forgive me. My life is rather complicated at present. Let me explain that Karl, though described as an interpreter, is really my bodyguard, escort, warder, and, you might say, resident spy. I don't doubt that he reports on me to Essenheim every day."

"And you have to give him something to report?"

"That's not far off the truth," Rudi said. "You see, the Prince Laureate and the Prime Minister will not care in the least if I show interest in a girl. To their minds, that is harmless. It is what they expect of a young man of my age. But talking to the Foreign Editor of the *Daily Intelligence* is quite another matter. That would make them deeply suspicious."

"That's all very well," Kate said as they turned into the local park, "but it's not very nice for me, is it? You said all those silly things at Susan's party, and you've got your arm round me now, and I'm nothing to you really but a way of getting to know my father."

Rudi looked contrite. "I'm sorry, Kate," he said. "And you are wrong. I like you very much. I liked you when I first saw you. I liked the way you talked to me. You

are independent. We don't have girls like you in Essenheim."

Kate felt herself relenting. She'd been meaning to
push Rudi's arm away, but she didn't. Then he said,
smiling, "But I ought to tell you that I am engaged
to be married."

Kate broke away from him at once. It was absurd
to feel as shattered as she did. It wasn't surprising,
was it, that he should be engaged? No, not at all. Yet
somehow it made his advances to her all the more
insulting.

"I saw my prospective bride in Florence, three weeks
ago. The wedding day, however, is still distant. She
is just ten years old."

"She's *what*?"

"Ten years old. She's heiress to a once-royal family—
and to a fortune. The match was made by my uncle.
Under Essenheim law, such engagements are legal and
binding."

"And what does *she* think about it?" Kate demanded.

"Nobody seems to care what she thinks about it. The
wedding cannot take place until she is sixteen. In the
meantime, so far as those around her are concerned,
it is none of her business. But now, dear Kate, I hope
you see one reason why I hope for change in Essenheim. I should like to marry to please myself."

"I should think so!" Kate declared. Then: "They can't
make you marry her, can they?"

"If I am to succeed to the princedom, yes. It would
be regarded as dishonorable if I were to break the
engagement—and financially disastrous, too. My uncle

26

would be under great pressure to name my cousin Friedrich as Crown Prince instead. Which would delight Dr. Stockhausen."

Suddenly, out of the corner of her eye, Kate saw the big old Rolls. It was crawling along the road that bounded the park, keeping them in view all the way.

"They're still watching you," she said. "Is it like that in Essenheim, too?"

"Not quite as bad. But bad enough."

"Seems to me it's a dog's life," said Kate.

"It *is* a dog's life. And I don't much look forward to being back in Essenheim. In a way, I would prefer to give it up, and find a nice girl of my own choice. Like you."

"I wonder if you really *would* like to give it up," Kate said. "I don't quite know what to believe."

"You can believe me about liking you."

Rudi gave her a slightly shamefaced grin. Kate preferred it to the stunning smile.

"All right," she said. "I will, for now. You can put your arm round me again, if it'll make Karl happy."

After lunch, Kate left Edward and Rudi alone for a couple of hours, during which time she sat at her desk in her own room and did an exceedingly small amount of homework. She wondered whether there would be a further public display of affection when Rudi left. But in fact he looked slightly downcast, and the leave-taking was cool and formal.

Kate stood beside Edward on the doorstep and watched the Rolls pull away. This time the chauffeur

27

was driving, and the interpreter, Karl, was sitting beside him. Rudi waved from the back window.

"Well, what do you think of him?" Kate asked her father as they went indoors.

"I haven't made up my mind. He's ambitious, and he certainly has lots of charm, but he's probably not too skilled at the power game. If he thinks he can twist the *Daily Intelligence* round his little finger, he's mistaken. However, from what he told me, it does seem as though things might start happening in Essenheim rather soon."

"Are you going to do as he asked and publish a report, so that this exile he talked about can launch his 'Free Essenheim' fund?"

"I might. But if I did, it would be purely on news values, not *because* he asked me."

"And will you take his word for what's going on?"

"Ah, well, that's another question. I don't like relying too much on what interested parties claim, however much they're acting in good faith. I shall put a reporter on it."

"How will *he* get his information?" Kate asked.

"He'll go to Essenheim, of course."

"I thought you told me they don't like visitors."

"Officially they don't, though I daresay the people are friendly enough. But if a keen young *Intelligence* reporter can't get into Essenheim, nobody can. I have just the right young man in mind—George Ormerod, who joined us last year from the north. . . . Speaking of right young men, what do *you* think of Rudi now?"

"I don't really know," Kate admitted. "First I didn't

28

like him, then I thought perhaps I did like him, then I thought again I didn't. And now I think perhaps I do. But I'm not sure."

"You may be seeing him again quite soon," said Edward. "I've asked him to come here next Tuesday and meet George." He paused meditatively. "I must say, Rudi wasn't exactly delighted when I told him I planned to put George on the story. That wasn't what he'd had in mind at all. I don't think he feels his mission to *me* was a total success. On the other hand"—Edward grinned—"he does seem to like seeing *you*."

"I wonder," said Kate, and sighed.

5

Kate couldn't stop thinking about Rudi during the days after he'd been to her house. She thought about him at all hours of the day, and once or twice she woke up in the night and thought about him some more.

The next Tuesday, the day he was due to come to the house again, Kate woke early with butterflies in her stomach. She went through the school day as if sleepwalking, and then hurried home. There was a small car in the drive, but no Rolls. Letting herself into the house, she heard male voices in the sitting room and pushed the door open.

Edward was there, but it wasn't Rudi with him. It was a stocky, serious-faced young man, with reddish hair and freckles, who got up from the sofa as she entered.

"Kate," Edward said, "this is my colleague George Ormerod. George, my daughter, Kate."

Kate's mind had been so full of Rudi that she'd forgotten she was going to meet George.

"Hello, Kate," George said. He extended a hand, rather awkwardly. Yes, she thought, he *would* be called

George. He seemed pleasant enough and not bad-looking, but a bit shy and, compared with a Prince, decidedly ordinary.

Without really thinking, Kate said, "I wouldn't have guessed you were on the *Daily Intelligence.*"

"Oh?" said George. "Why not?"

"Well, I've met *Intelligence* reporters before. They're terribly bright—you can hardly look at them for the shine in their eyes—and rather classy. You can tell at a glance that they went to Oxford or Cambridge—" Then she realized that she was saying the wrong things and added lamely, "Of course, I expect *you're* madly brilliant, too."

"I'm not madly brilliant," said George, "and I didn't go to Oxford or Cambridge. But I *am* a reporter. I trained on a local paper."

"George is a real professional," said Edward. "That's why I'm putting him on the Essenheim story. I don't want clever, witty essays by a bright young man from Oxford or Cambridge. I just want to find out what's happening. . . . And, by the way, I hope Rudi will turn up before too long. In the meantime, why don't you two have a look at this while I go into the next room and make a phone call?"

Edward had brought a book from the *Daily Intelligence* library called *Countries of Central Europe.* It was quite a fat book, but only one pair of pages was devoted to Essenheim. Kate and George sat side by side, poring over it.

Kate had the more interesting page. There were three pictures on it, in grainy black and white. One showed a marvelously complicated Gothic castle, sprouting from a hilltop like some monstrous plant and throwing out towers and battlements as it went. "Essenheim Castle," said the caption. The second was a scene of cobbled streets, overhanging houses and little old-fashioned shops. "Essenheim Town," said the caption with equal brevity. The last showed a distant prospect of a small town clinging to a hillside, and had the comparatively wordy caption: "Essenheim Town from across the Esel River."

While Kate studied the pictures, George had been reading the text. "It doesn't tell you much," he said. "Fifteen thousand people. One town, called Essenheim like the country, and four small villages. Lots of mountains. Ruler, Prince Ferdinand Franz Josef the Third."

"That's Rudi's Uncle Ferdy," said Kate.

"Here's an interesting bit, though. Seems they have their own language, Essenheimisch, but it's not much used outside the home; most of the people speak English. Fascinating, eh?"

"Fascinating," Kate agreed. But what she was really thinking was *Where's Rudi?*

"If I've time before I go there," said George seriously, "I shall try to learn some Essenheimisch. It always makes a good impression if you know a little of the mother tongue."

Edward came back from his telephone call. Half an hour went by, but there was still no Rudi. George and Edward exchanged newspaper gossip. Kate sat mostly silent, feeling increasingly let down. Finally Edward looked at his watch and sighed. "The fellow's not com-

32

ing," he said. "We may as well give up."

Kate said, "Do you mean you'll drop Essenheim?"

Edward said, "Certainly not. Far from it."

George said, "It means a bit more work for me, that's all."

Kate didn't know whether to be indignant or worried. If Rudi could have come and hadn't bothered, she felt that indignation was appropriate. But what if he'd been prevented from coming?

"Tomorrow, Kate," said Edward, "why don't you call the Essenheim Consulate and see what you can find out?"

"That's my job, really," said George.

"No, it's not," Edward told him. "This is a case for discretion. Rudi took a risk by getting in touch with me. It might not help him at all to have inquiries made by the *Daily Intelligence.*"

Then he poured drinks for himself and George, and after ten more minutes, during which there was still no sign of Rudi, they went off to the office in George's five-year-old Volkswagen.

Kate was quite willing to call the Essenheim Consulate. Its number was in the telephone book, which also told her its address—a rather modest one in South Kensington. But although she tried at intervals during the next two days, no one ever answered the phone. On Friday, the first day of a long midterm weekend, Kate didn't have to go to school. And halfway through the morning, after several unsuccessful attempts, she got an answer at last.

33

"Essenheim Consulate," said a grating male voice. It added, in a surly tone, "What do you want?"

"I'd like to speak to the Consul, please," Kate said.

"*I* am the Consul. Who are you?"

"I'm a friend of Prince Rudi's. I wondered if it was possible to get in touch with him."

"Prince Rudolf has many friends. Please give your name."

Kate hesitated for a moment. She wasn't sure whether it would be in Rudi's interest for her to say who she was. Before she had decided the voice went on, suspiciously, "Not the young lady his Highness went to see on Saturday?"

"Yes," said Kate.

"Prince Rudolf is no longer in the country. He has been recalled to Essenheim."

"Oh!" Kate gasped in dismay. "Did he leave any messages?"

"He left no messages for anyone," said the voice, still surly. "I have nothing more to tell you. Good-bye." And the Essenheim Consul hung up.

Ten minutes later Edward came down for breakfast, rubbing his eyes. Kate reported, ruefully, on her efforts. Edward pulled a face. "That seems to finish Rudi as a source of preliminary information," he said. "George will have to find out what he can, where he can."

"Is that all you have to say?" Kate asked plaintively.

"Don't look so forlorn," Edward said. He took his daughter's hand. "You hardly know Rudi. A couple of weeks ago you weren't even aware that he existed."

"But what will become of him?" Kate asked. "He

may be in trouble. And I don't like the sound of that Prime Minister, Dr. Stockhausen."

"I shouldn't worry too much. Rudi *is* a Prince, and Essenheim's not entirely a dictatorship. And I formed the impression that that young man can look after himself."

"I hope you're right," Kate said; and then, wistfully, "I wonder if I'll ever see him again."

"Frankly, my dear," said Edward, "I wouldn't count on it."

6

⟡⟨ ⟩⟡

In the next few weeks Kate heard nothing from or about Rudi. At first she hoped each day for a letter from Essenheim to explain why he hadn't had a chance to get in touch before he left. Slowly this hope faded, but her interest in Rudi and in Essenheim itself refused to fade with it. The pictures of the Gothic castle and the small hilly town kept coming into her mind. She had an occasional daydream in which she was wandering through the grounds of Essenheim Castle when suddenly Rudi appeared round a corner. He was as handsome as ever and had been writing to her every day, but his mail had been intercepted by the odious Dr. Stockhausen. "Kate," he said in the daydream, "dear Kate, there has never been a moment when you were not in my thoughts. . . ."

While Rudi was absent, George was very much present. The *Daily Intelligence* had decided that he should finish a series of articles he was doing on London local politics before he went to Essenheim. He found reasons for coming twice to Edward's house, and seemed to enjoy talking to Kate. Before the second of these occasions, Edward said to Kate, "I bet he'll ask you for a date." He won his bet.

Kate obligingly let George take her to a movie. She liked him well enough, but he suffered from the disadvantage of not being Rudi. Afterward they went to a coffee shop, where George outlined his views on life in general and journalism in particular. Kate threw in remarks at random when she felt they were called for. On one occasion, when she fell silent, he asked what she was thinking, and Kate, caught off balance, confessed that her thoughts were on Essenheim, though she had tact enough not to mention Rudi.

"I think about Essenheim a lot myself," said George. "I'll be going in about three weeks' time, I expect, though we still haven't fixed a date. Some of the fellows are jealous. They'd *all* like to go to Essenheim."

"I think I'm jealous too," said Kate.

Next day George called her from the office. "How'd you like to learn some Essenheimisch?" he inquired. "There aren't any classes in London, but I've found a Dr. Falkstadt, an exile, whom I think Rudi mentioned to your dad. It seems he'd be willing to take a couple of pupils, two evenings a week. I'd like to get a smattering of it before I go. How about coming with me?"

For the first time, Kate found herself responding warmly to George.

"Yes, please!" she said. "I'd love to!"

Dr. Theodor Falkstadt took George and Kate up several flights of stairs to the tiny apartment he rented at the top of a house at Blackheath, in southeast London. He was a small, elderly man, completely bald, with a gentle voice and expression, and he was neatly dressed in clothes that had reached a state of terminal shabbiness.

"Gracious young lady and gallant gentleman," he said, "I shall be delighted to teach you what I can, in so short a time, of the language of my country. I have in fact two other pupils, both Essenheimers. But let me impress upon you that I am not by profession a language teacher. I do a little teaching because, to be frank, the money is welcome. As a foreigner in London, I do not find it easy to earn my daily bread."

"Why did you leave Essenheim?" asked George.

"I had, shall we say, a slight disagreement with the Prime Minister, Dr. Stockhausen. I ventured to criticize his authoritarian regime. Next day it was suggested to me that I might find it convenient to leave the country. I thought it wise to accept the suggestion. And now, I hear the doorbell. In a minute you will meet my other two pupils."

The other two pupils were a plump, round-faced, cheerful young man in a dark-red velvet jacket, and a tall girl with a very pale face, a severe expression, and long straight black hair parted in the middle. Dr. Falkstadt introduced them as Aleksi and Sonia.

"They speak English already, of course," he said, "as most Essenheimers do. They come to me to improve it, and perhaps to some extent because we Essenheimers must stick together. I think we shall form an effective group. Aleksi and Sonia will speak only English, and when you two have learned a little Essenheimisch, you must try to speak only that."

"And what do you do, Aleksi?" George asked.

"I am a poet," Aleksi said. "Essenheim has as yet no national poet. That is my opportunity. I have been studying the works of the great English poets. Soon I shall return to my country. My aim will be to write great poetry in Essenheimisch. I should like to be Essenheim's Shakespeare, Milton, and Wordsworth, all three."

"That sounds quite a program," said George.

"And what about you, Sonia?" asked Kate.

"I am a revolutionary."

There was a moment's surprised silence. Then George said, "That's not usually a way of making a living."

"Sonia teaches in the University of Essenheim," said Dr. Falkstadt.

"That is true," said Sonia. "I have been on a year's sabbatical. Soon I go back, in readiness for the revolution. Last year I shook the dust of Essenheim from my feet. But this year the dust will be back on my feet with a vengeance! The old regime will be overthrown and the university will serve the people!"

Kate could see that George's professional interest was mounting.

"Who will lead the revolution?" he asked. "Prince Rudi?"

"Prince Rudi? Certainly not! He is a mere aristocrat.

I spit on aristocrats. But I shall tell you nothing more. I have heard about you. You are a lackey of the capitalist press. I do not trust you!"

Dr. Falkstadt intervened, looking anxious. "I think that's enough of that subject," he said. "We are not here to discuss politics. You all pay me for this lesson, and I must earn my money. Now, George and Kate, let me give you books."

He handed each of them a battered copy of a young children's storybook, printed in heavy, old-fashioned Gothic type.

"It is not ideal," he said. "It has many misprints. There is only one printing house in Essenheim, and it is not very good. That will not matter greatly, as I teach by the direct method. But first of all I wish you to see Essenheimisch in print. Let me now read you the story, and you will follow the action from the pictures. After that, as their next practice, Aleksi and Sonia will tell you the story in English. Thus we shall kill two birds with one stone."

The story was easy enough to understand. It was about a small black sheep that strayed from the flock and was found and revived by a kindly shepherd. Having gravely read it aloud, Dr. Falkstadt turned to Sonia. "Now," he said, "you tell us the first part of the story in English."

"I refuse," said Sonia. "It is bourgeois sexist racist ageist elitist fascist propaganda. I spit on it."

"Seems to me," said George as he drove Kate back to her home in Hammersmith, "that Aleksi and Sonia

are a couple of crackpots. Do you suppose that Essenheim's full of crackpots?"

"I wouldn't know," said Kate. "But one way or another, I think you're going to have an interesting time."

7

Kate and George competed, in a friendly way, to see who could learn more Essenheimisch in the time available. Kate had always been good at languages. George didn't have her gift but was a hard worker, so their progress was roughly equal. Twice a week they drove to Highgate for conversation with Dr. Falkstadt and his other two pupils. In a surprisingly short time they could express themselves in halting, limited but quite comprehensible sentences. Dr. Falkstadt was delighted with them.

Meanwhile, Kate had her seventeenth birthday and the summer term at her school drew toward a close. On the morning of the last day of term, Kate came into the kitchen to find that Edward, bleary eyed and dressing gowned, was there before her. He was drinking coffee and leafing through the pile of newspapers that had descended, as usual, on the Milbanks' doormat.

"Hello!" she said. "What's up?"

"I am," said Edward.

"I can see that. But it's only half past seven. I can't

42

remember when you were last around before double figures."

"Kate," said Edward, "there's a funny twist to the Essenheim story. You won't like it, I'm afraid."

Kate sat down opposite him, feeling apprehensive.

"You remember," Edward said, "that when you called the Essenheim Consulate you were told Rudi had gone home?"

"Yes, of course. How could I forget?"

"Well, now, the *Daily Intelligence* has a correspondent in Serenia, the country next door to Essenheim, and the correspondent himself, like all correspondents, has various sources of information. One of these happens to be near the Essenheim frontier. And he's been picking up some curious stuff on Radio Essenheim."

"That's the first I've heard of Radio Essenheim," Kate said.

"Well, Radio Essenheim is actually just one radio transmitter that's always breaking down. And when it *is* working the broadcasts can be heard only a few miles beyond the frontier. And most of the time they just play last year's pop music. But anyway, our correspondent's man has heard on the radio that Prince Rudi hasn't returned to Essenheim."

"What?" Kate was aghast.

"He hasn't got back to base. Or so their radio says."

"What's happened to him, then?"

"I don't know. I wish I did."

"And what are the Essenheim authorities doing about it?"

43

"Nothing, apparently. It's being presented as a desertion. The old Prince, it's said, sent Rudi on this Grand Tour, and Rudi repaid his kindness by deserting him for wine, women, and song."

"Do you believe that's what's happened?" asked Kate.

"How would I know? I'm merely reporting what Radio Essenheim says. And I haven't told you all of it yet. This nonreturn of Rudi's was quite a while ago."

"Six weeks," said Kate, who remembered exactly.

"Right. It was some time before our source in Serenia happened to pick this up. He doesn't spend his days with his ear glued to Radio Essenheim. And by the time he latched onto it, the story had developed further. It seems that the old Prince Laureate has decided, or been persuaded, that this means he should chuck Rudi and name his cousin Friedrich as Crown Prince. Friedrich will be proclaimed heir to the throne as soon as he's eighteen, in a few weeks' time."

"Oho," said Kate. "But what if Rudi turns up before then?"

"I have no idea. But there has to be a Crown Prince to secure the throne; otherwise if anything happens to the old boy there's a strong chance that the country falls into anarchy. And the Prince Laureate rates the continuance of the monarchy above all else. Hence the proclamation of Friedrich."

"I hope nothing dreadful has happened," said Kate unhappily.

"There's certainly a curious smell about the affair,"

44

said Edward. "I think *somebody* is up to something peculiar."

"What are you suggesting?" Kate asked.

"I'm not exactly suggesting anything, just wondering. Didn't Rudi say the interpreter was there to keep an eye on him?"

"Bodyguard, escort, warder, and resident spy," said Kate, remembering. "Rudi also told me that Dr. Stockhausen would be delighted if Friedrich stepped into his shoes."

"Well, then, what if Stockhausen wanted to get Rudi out of the way? And succeeded?"

"If *I* said that," said Kate, "you'd accuse me of being melodramatic."

"All right," said Edward. "Point taken. However, I was interested enough to get onto James Higgins about Rudi's departure. Getting information from him is like getting blood out of a stone. So far as the Foreign Office is concerned, Rudi left London Airport all those weeks ago on a scheduled flight to Serenia, intending to change there for Essenheim. What he may have done since then is nobody's business. Least of all, James gave me to understand, that of the *Daily Intelligence.*"

"Did anyone actually see him go?"

"Apparently not. James's department would have seen him off, but the offer was declined because Rudi's visit was a private one. He was traveling under his family name, Rudolf Hohlberg."

"Could he still be in this country, then?"

"Unlikely. His name was on the passenger list. But he could have gone back to Essenheim, in spite of what

45

the radio says, and been spirited away out of sight. He could be languishing in the dungeons of Essenheim Castle."

"He couldn't. Oh, he *couldn't!* Could he?"

"Don't be upset. I don't really think so. But there's no end to the possibilities."

"So what is the *Daily Intelligence* going to *do*?"

"We talked about it a good deal in the office last night. We could, of course, run a story on the strength of what we have already—a 'mystery of the missing prince' affair. But that would blow the whole thing and get the popular press onto it. At the moment nobody but us seems to know. I think instead we shall try to do a proper job on this. We've brought George's departure forward; he's off to Essenheim later this week. In the meantime, we're getting in touch with everyone Rudi is known to have seen during his tour. It may still turn out that he simply got tired of the whole scene, threw in his hand, and has gone to stay with some minor royalty on a country estate somewhere in Europe. If so, we'll trace him. If not . . . well, it may be quite a story we're onto."

"It's more than a newspaper story to me," said Kate dismally.

"I know it is, my dear," said Edward. He rubbed a sympathetic though unshaven cheek against hers. "That's why I wanted you to know what had happened as soon as possible. And now, if you'll forgive me, I'll totter back to bed. I wasn't home until nearly four, and I'm not as good as I used to be at managing on three and a half hours of sleep."

8

That afternoon Kate walked part of the way home from school with Susan Baker. It was the end of the school year as well as the end of the summer term; Kate didn't have to go back until mid-September, which was eight weeks away. She'd just parted company with Susan when there was a squeal of brakes and a car drew up precipitately a few yards ahead of her. The door on the passenger side flew open, and a bearded man called from the driver's seat, urgently, "Kate!"

Kate, startled, went up to the car.

"Jump in!" the driver told her.

It took her a second or two to recognize him. The bearded driver was Rudi.

Kate didn't stop to think. She got into the car, which was a newish Triumph. Rudi leaned over to kiss her, then steered instantly into the traffic. The whole incident had taken less than a minute.

"Where are we going?" Kate asked.

Rudi was driving rather fast in the busy streets, nipping in and out between other vehicles.

"We are going to your house. I shall talk very rapidly

with your father. Meanwhile, you will pack a bag. You will do it quickly, in five minutes, no more. I hope you have a passport."

"Yes, I have a passport. But why do I need it? Where am I going?"

"You are going to Essenheim."

"Thank you for telling me," said Kate. "But how do you know I want to go there? And what's my father going to say? And what will I do for money? And what—"

"Be calm," Rudi said. "All shall be arranged. I shall speak to your father. He will not refuse a request from me."

Kate thought her father quite capable of refusing a request from anybody except perhaps herself. But what she said to Rudi was "He won't be at home. He goes to work before this time. He'll be at the *Daily Intelligence* office by now."

Rudi seemed momentarily taken aback, but then retorted, "Has the *Daily Intelligence* no telephones?"

"Of course it has. But are you going to spring a thing like that on him over the phone? Anyway, as I said before, how do you know I want to go to Essenheim?" In spite of her daydreams and her envy of George, she suddenly found the prospect of a trip to a little-known, faraway country rather alarming.

"Kate," said Rudi, "it is very urgent, very important, and there is no time to lose. You *must* come to Essenheim. In any case, how could you refuse? You are invited. My sister, Princess Anni, invites you. I convey

48

the invitation to you now on her behalf. It is not usual to turn down a royal invitation. In my country it would be considered unbecoming conduct on the part of a subject."

"I thought you didn't believe in that royalty stuff," Kate said. "And anyway, I'm not a subject of yours! Or of Princess Anni's. I'd never even heard of her until this moment."

"It's true you're not a subject." Rudi turned his face aside long enough to give her a charming smile. "But won't you come as a friend?"

"How long do you want me to go for? And what about money? I've got just seven pounds and sixty pence in the bank."

"There will be no expense. You will stay as a guest at Essenheim Castle for a week, perhaps two weeks. Then it will be for you to decide whether you wish to stay longer. I am not abducting you, Kate." He gave her the charming smile again. "Look, we have arrived at your house. I have remembered well the way, haven't I? Jump out. Open the door, quickly. Good. . . . Now, where is the telephone and what is the number?"

Kate told him the number and stood by as he dialed.

"Don't wait here!" he instructed her. "Get your passport and pack your bag. Go on. Go!"

Kate hurried upstairs to her room. With part of her mind she stood outside herself, watching herself throw things into a suitcase, wondering why she was doing it, and not really believing in the situation at all. She

49

had just finished packing and taken her passport from a drawer when Rudi's voice came commandingly up the stairs: "Kate! Kate! Speak to your father!"

Rudi wasn't looking too pleased. Kate wondered if Edward had objected to the trip. But soon it was clear that he hadn't. "This is a mad caper, isn't it?" he said cheerfully on the phone. He didn't sound as if he thought it impossibly mad, though. As a Foreign Editor he lived in a world in which people were forever going abroad at a moment's notice. To him it was a normal way of life. He went on, "You really do want to go, don't you, Kate?"

"Yes," said Kate, although until she heard herself say it she hadn't been quite sure.

"All right, good. Now listen. Rudi says Essenheim is as peaceful as ever and this trip will just be a holiday for you. But I'm sending George along and I want you to keep in touch with him while you're there, understand?"

"George?" said Kate. "I thought he wasn't going until later in the week."

"Well, I've just revised his travel plans. You and Rudi will not depart without him, got that?"

"Yes," said Kate glumly. The thought of George as a member of the party was something of a dampener.

"Okay. Have a good time. And I hope you're not away too long. I shall miss your cooking."

Kate knew that was his way of saying he'd miss *her*. She might have said that she'd miss *him*, but Rudi had picked up her bag and was alternately looking at his watch and jingling his car keys impatiently. "Good-bye," she said, and put the receiver down. The next minute she was being tugged out to the car by Rudi.

"This isn't the way to the airport," Kate said two or three minutes later.

"We're not going to the airport."

Kate said, "Listen, Rudi, will you *please* put me in the picture? Here I am, dashing off to regions unknown with nothing but a toothbrush—well, *practically* nothing but a toothbrush—and you've hardly told me the first thing about it. Why are we in such a hurry? Where have you been these last six weeks? What about George? What—"

"One question at a time, please," Rudi said.

"All right. Just where are we going?"

"I've told you. We're going to Essenheim."

"Then *how* are we going, if we're not on our way to the airport?"

"We are going mainly by road. We shall cross the Channel from Dover to Calais and drive through France and Switzerland to Serenia. There we shall catch a plane to Essenheim. It's all quite simple."

"How long will it take?"

"Three days, all being well."

"But I thought we were in a tearing hurry. So why aren't we going by air all the way?"

"The hurry is not a hurry to arrive in Essenheim," Rudi said. "We are in a hurry to get out of England, because it is possible that we are being pursued. And we are not going by air because I see the airport as a danger point for us. It will be safer by sea, I hope."

Kate's heart bumped. "Pursued!" she echoed. "Who by?"

"By Karl and Josef. You may remember Karl. He accompanied me to your house on my previous visit."

"I do remember," Kate said. Karl, the "interpreter." She had not liked the look of Karl.

"Josef I think you have not met," said Rudi. "I hope you never do. Josef makes Karl look like a Victorian maiden aunt."

"But why?" demanded Kate. "Why, why, why?"

"Let me return to your earlier question," Rudi said. "You asked where I had been these past weeks. The answer is that I have been in a farmhouse in a remote part of Somerset. Imprisoned. That is why I have the beard."

"Imprisoned!" Kate's heart bumped again. "You mean you were kidnapped?"

"Precisely. On the way to the airport. It was very simple. Young Stockhausen—the son of the Essenheim Consul here, and nephew of our Prime Minister—was to drive me there in his own car, which is the one we are in now. Soon after picking me up, he drove into an enclosed yard, where Karl and Josef had already parked another car. They came over to us, and when I asked what was going on, Josef said, 'This,' and hit me on the head. I gather that Albrecht Stockhausen went on to the airport in the other car, and flew to Serenia in my name. Karl drove me to Somerset in this one, and Josef took the other car from the airport and joined us there."

Kate said, "I can't believe it! Kidnapped! In England!" And then: "How did they treat you?"

"They treated me well, but I was very bored. Karl was bored too, and probably told me more than he should have."

"What were they aiming to achieve?"

"They'd have held me until Dr. Stockhausen's protégé, my cousin Friedrich, was installed as Crown Prince, and the Stockhausens' future power assured. Then I expect they'd have let me go. If I'd gone home and told the tale after that, it would have been my word against everybody else's, and no one would have believed me. I have, I'm afraid, some reputation for irresponsibility. Anyway, I've escaped just in time, and all being well I shall put matters right."

"How *did* you escape, Rudi?"

"That was quite simple, too, when the opportunity came. Through the window of the room where I was confined, I saw Josef set off in his car. When Karl came to my room I hit *him* on the head. With a leg screwed off the bed, as a matter of fact. It gave me great satisfaction. Then I took his keys and young Stockhausen's car, and here we are!"

"Well!" said Kate. "When you put it like that it *does* sound simple."

Rudi said, "I don't know how much time I had in hand. Possibly it wasn't long before Josef returned. Then they'd be after me. However, there are only the two of them—so far as I know they have no organization. Don't worry, dear Kate. Prepare to enjoy your holiday."

"Did you tell my father you'd been kidnapped?" Kate asked.

"No. There was not time."

"I think it was a bit sneaky not to tell him. Even *he* might not have been keen to let me come if he'd known about that. It's a wonder I'm not scared out of my wits."

"I had no wish to worry your father. And I did desire his consent, or rather his goodwill. That's why I agreed to take George." Rudi frowned. "I hope that will not spoil the party, so to speak. I have not met this George. What is he like?"

"Oh, George is all right. He's not the most exciting person in the world."

"Good. I'm glad of that. I must try to fill that role myself."

"Well, you have a head start," said Kate. "It's not everyone who can involve a girl in a nice exciting pursuit by a couple of thugs. Anyway, where are we picking up George?"

"At the home of a friend and compatriot of mine, in Blackheath."

"Dr. Falkstadt!"

"Yes, indeed. Dr. Falkstadt. Obviously you know him?"

Kate realized that Rudi was unaware that she'd been taking language lessons. She told him so, in Essenheimisch. He looked at her with surprise, then commented,

"Not bad. Not bad at all. You have a good accent. They will like that in Essenheim."

When they arrived at the house in Blackheath where Dr. Falkstadt had his apartment, Rudi rang the doorbell three or four times in rapid succession. Dr. Falkstadt had obviously been waiting for them. He flung open the door.

"My dear Prince!" he cried, embracing Rudi warmly. "Come in! I have been telephoned by the *Daily Intelligence*, and I understand our friend George will be here within five minutes." He added sadly, "I am about to lose all my pupils. Aleksi and Sonia will also be on their way to Essenheim in two or three days' time."

The five minutes became ten, and Rudi grew visibly impatient before a somewhat flustered George arrived. He was introduced to Rudi, who greeted him with chilly politeness. Farewells were said to Dr. Falkstadt, and Rudi pointedly opened the back door of the car for George. Kate retained her front seat.

The journey from London to Dover was slightly fraught. Rudi drove alarmingly fast and was lucky not to be picked up for speeding. Either in anxiety over possible pursuit or resentment at the unwanted presence of George, he was silent most of the time. George sat in the back, equally silent and writing steadily in a notebook.

It was raining when they reached Dover. There was some delay over the formalities, and a wait in line to drive onto the ferry. Rudi looked at his watch several times, and at intervals glanced anxiously back along the growing line of cars. Only when the crossing had begun did he relax. Then he said quietly to Kate, "Karl and Josef are not on board. We are safe now. In three days' time we shall arrive at the castle. You will be happy there."

Kate hoped he was right. For the time being she was stunned by the rush of events. She couldn't quite believe she was on her way to Essenheim.

9

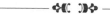

They stopped for the night at an inn a bit beyond Calais. The next morning Rudi appeared without his beard, looking more handsome than ever. Shortly after breakfast, the three of them got back into the car and set out for the Swiss border.

Kate didn't really enjoy the journey. It was soon clear that Rudi and George had not taken to each other. Rudi again directed George into the backseat, and drove very fast all morning. After lunch Rudi accepted an offer from George to take a turn at the wheel, but Kate's relief was succeeded by embarrassment when Rudi expected her to sit beside him in the back. Not wishing to make George so obviously the odd man out, Kate diplomatically pleaded that sitting in the back always made her carsick, and resumed her front seat.

Before long Rudi began to make remarks about George's sedate style of driving. George seemed oblivious to these comments, but put in an earnest request that they should all practice conversation in Essenheimisch. Rudi agreed with obvious reluctance.

On the second day Rudi kept George firmly in the

back all the time, while he himself talked quietly in English to Kate in the front. By the end of that day it was hard to guess whether Rudi was more irritated with George or George with Rudi.

On the third morning, in brilliant sunshine, they drove out of Switzerland into Serenia along a straight, smooth highway with vantage points at frequent intervals for viewing the spectacular mountain scenery. In early afternoon they left the highway and took to smaller, winding lanes, passing through villages of bright wooden houses carved like music boxes. They began to descend, leaving the snowcapped peaks behind them; the landscape became grassy and wooded, hilly rather than mountainous. And at last they came to a road sign, of elegant design and typography, pointing to EAST SERENIAN AIRPORT, 3 KILOMETERS.

The airport had a parking lot with room for a thousand cars, and holding perhaps half a dozen. Rudi drove straight on past a gleaming terminal building; beyond it a sleek Air Serenia jet sat on the tarmac. Rudi proceeded around the perimeter of the huge parking lot.

"This is the civilized end of the field," he explained. "They've left *our* terminal at the other end, where it was before all this progress."

At the farthest corner of the airfield was a wooden shack, in front of which stood a small, two-propeller aircraft—a type that Kate could not identify. Over the door of the shack and on the side of the plane was printed, in Gothic lettering, ROYAL ESSENHEIM AIRWAYS, and beside this inscription was a bunch of grapes. Neither shack nor aircraft looked as if it had been painted lately.

"Look well on this," said Rudi. "This is our one and only plane, all ready—I hope—to fly on its one and only route, between here and Essenheim. It's just a hundred and fifty kilometers. With a bit of luck, I daresay we shall make it."

Half a dozen men sat on a long bench in front of the shack. They were eating out of paper packages and passing a bottle around among them. Three wore dirty overalls; the other three wore equally dirty purple uniforms with wings on the chest and rings around the sleeves. All six got up. One of the uniformed men, a spiderlike figure with a short torso but unusually long arms and legs, stepped forward and extended a hand.

"Hello, Highness," he said cheerfully. "This is a nice surprise. We'd been told you were never coming back. Mind you, I didn't believe it. I knew you'd be along one of these days."

"Hello, Fritzi," Rudi said. "Good to see you."

"You've timed it well, Highness. We'll be taking off pretty soon."

"I know your departure time as well as you do, Fritzi," Rudi said.

The six men turned out to be two thirds of the entire staff of Royal Essenheim Airways. Fritzi was the Chief Pilot; there were also the Deputy Chief (and only other) Pilot, the Flight Engineer, two mechanics, and the Airport Director, whose broom was leaning against the shack. It appeared that in Essenheim itself there were

59

two more mechanics and another Airport Director.

"Excuse us while we finish our snack, Highness," said Fritzi. He dug the Airport Director in the ribs. "Pass us that bottle!"

Kate whispered to Rudi, "I don't think he's quite sober."

"Of course he's not!" said Rudi. He added, without bothering to drop his voice, "He's as drunk as a lord."

"Drunk as a prince, we say in Essenheim," remarked Fritzi.

"Watch it, Fritzi!" Rudi warned him, grinning. "If I were Prince Laureate, that'd be high treason. You'd finish up in the bargain basement!"

"What's the bargain basement?" asked George. All six men burst out laughing.

"It's our name for the dungeons of Essenheim Castle," said Rudi.

While Fritzi and his friends finished their snack, Rudi helped George and Kate transfer their few pieces of luggage to the hold of the little plane. Rudi himself had only the clothes he stood up in.

"We'll leave the car right here," he said. "It belongs to Albrecht Stockhausen. Heaven knows where he is now, but retrieving it is *his* problem."

A second Air Serenia jet had landed on the main runway and was taxiing toward the Serenian terminal building.

"That's today's flight from London just arriving," the Airport Director told Kate. "Sometimes there's a passenger for us to take on to Essenheim, but nobody

60

bothers to tell us beforehand. They think we're a one-horse outfit."

"We *are* a one-horse outfit," said Fritzi contentedly.

A minute later the telephone rang in the Essenheim Airways shack. The Airport Director put down a half-eaten sandwich and shambled inside, still chewing. He emerged and shouted, "Hold it, Fritzi! That was the main terminal. There's two people from London for us!"

Rudi exclaimed sharply in Essenheimisch. "Surely it can't be Karl and Josef!" he said to Kate. "They wouldn't have the nerve to follow us this far!"

Kate thought he didn't sound quite sure. But her alarm lasted only a moment. The Airport Director read out the names he'd jotted down on a scrap of paper. "It's a Countess Zackendorf and a Mr. Wandervogel," he said.

"Oh, it's Aleksi and Sonia!" Kate declared in relief. "I'd forgotten they were coming back to Essenheim!"

"I know them," Rudi said, sounding equally relieved. "Sonia makes a lot of noise, but they're both harmless. Let's get aboard and pick our seats."

He maneuvered himself into the seat next to Kate. George sat behind them as he had done in the car. Some minutes later, with the engines already revving up, Sonia and Aleksi were hurried into the plane.

Kate was relieved that the copilot, who appeared to be sober and competent, was in the pilot's seat. There was some cross talk with ground control on the radio, and the plane taxied out to the runway and took off. The ground reared up sharply, first on one side and then on the other. Kate felt apprehensive; she'd only flown once before, and it hadn't been quite like this.

"It's all right," Rudi said as the plane leveled out and headed down the valley. "They know what they're doing."

At a point where two rivers flowed together, the plane took a sharp turn left and headed up a different valley toward high ground.

"We're in the Esel Valley now," Rudi told Kate. "We just follow it up into the hills and we come to Essenheim."

Kate looked down with interest, first at broad meadows and lush farming country, then at increasingly steep riverside slopes covered with vines. High mountaintops could once again be glimpsed in the distance. At one point there was a series of dams and small lakes.

"That's the Serenian hydroelectric plant." Rudi said. And a few minutes later: "See the village down there? That's on the frontier. We're passing into Essenheim airspace now."

The radio crackled. Fritzi turned to speak to Rudi. "Are we to tell them you're coming, Highness?"

"No, Fritzi. The news would get to the Prime Minister before it got to the Prince Laureate. In fact, it might not get to the Prince at all. What if I were arrested?"

"All right, Highness," Fritzi said. "We'll just land quietly and leave it to you."

In another ten minutes they were above the town

of Essenheim. Kate could see even from above that it was a steep little place, divided by chasms where swift mountain streams ran into each other, crisscrossed by bridges. Pink-roofed houses clung to the slopes. Near the town center, soaring skyward from a crag, was the dynamic shape of the high Gothic castle—Kate recognized it at once from the picture in the reference book.

"Am I actually staying *there*?" she asked incredulously.

"You are. As my guest. Or rather, as the guest of my sister Anni. She will like you. You will like her."

"What about George?"

Rudi frowned. "Oh, yes, George. Out of courtesy to your father I would ask George to be a guest at the castle too, but it wouldn't be the best vantage point for him. The authorities don't like journalists. He shall stay at the Ritz-Albany Hotel, where he will be comfortable. It used to be Frau Schmidt's boardinghouse. Indeed, it still is."

"I must keep in touch with George," said Kate. "My father insisted on it."

"You will have little difficulty in maintaining contact with George. The telephone service works most of the time, and if it fails there are messengers."

The airstrip was now in sight below. It was a tiny field located disconcertingly between a deep chasm and a cemetery. But the little aircraft dived straight in to make a safe, smooth landing.

"Your Highness, gracious young ladies and gallant gentlemen," proclaimed Fritzi importantly, "I am

63

pleased to announce that today's Flight Number One of Royal Essenheim Airways has just landed at Essenheim Airport. Kindly remain in your seats with seat belts fastened until the aircraft comes to a halt."

10

The Essenheim airport was somewhat grander than
Essenheim Airways' establishment in Serenia. There
were two shacks instead of one. Over the first shack
was the legend

**ROYAL ESSENHEIM CUSTOMS
AND IMMIGRATION**

and against a doorpost leaned a somewhat shaggy official in a coarse purple uniform. On one shoulder tab
were the words ROYAL ESSENHEIM CUSTOMS and on
the other ROYAL ESSENHEIM IMMIGRATION. He advanced, grinning.

"Well, Fritzi, who've you brought us?" And then:
"Why, Highness, it's you! Welcome back to Essenheim!"

He turned to the other passengers and put on an
official expression.

"Your passports, please," he said.

Sonia and Aleksi produced passports with covers of
purple cardboard, and were waved on their way. The
official looked dubiously at Kate's and George's British

passports. "There is no admission without an Essenheim visa," he told them.

"They are my guests," said Rudi coldly. "Kindly allow
them to proceed."

The official shrugged his shoulders, winked at Fritzi,
and retreated toward his shack.

"For a country that doesn't like foreigners," George
remarked, "Essenheim doesn't seem to have very vigi-
lant watchdogs."

"S-s-s-sh!" said Kate.

The other shack, the Airport Director's office, was
empty. "He'll be out at one of the wine cellars," said
Rudi. "But we can use his telephone, that's the main
thing. If it's working, of course."

The telephone was an old-fashioned upright type
with a separate earpiece. Kate watched as Rudi un-
hooked it.

"Hello! Exchange!" he said; and then, at intervals: "Hello! . . . Hello! . . . Hello! . . . This is Prince
Rudi. . . . I said it's Prince Rudi! . . . Just put me
through to my uncle, will you? Yes, the Prince!"

There was a brief silence. Rudi looked up and winked
at Kate. Then: "Hello, Uncle, it's me, Rudi. . . . Yes,
I'm here in Essenheim. At the airport. I've just
arrived. . . . Yes, I know about Friedrich. Now that
I'm back you can send him packing. . . . Yes, I know
your conditions, and I've met them. . . . Yes, she's perfectly suitable. She's ideal. You'll love her. . . . Oh,
never mind what Dr. Stockhausen says. You're the
ruler, aren't you? . . . Yes, I'm overjoyed, too. Yes,
please have a guest room prepared. . . . Yes, my love

66

to Anni. . . . Yes, send the car round right away. . . . Good-bye, Uncle, I'll see you in a few minutes."

Rudi hung up, grinning. "There!" he said. "All fixed up!"

"Is the guest room for me?" inquired Kate.

"Yes."

"And what am I perfectly suitable for?"

"You'll learn before long, dear Kate."

"What about the rest of us?" asked George.

Rudi looked around at the others. "Let's see. When the car comes, George, Kate and I will drop you off at the Ritz-Albany Hotel. Now, Aleksi, my old friend . . . ?"

"I shall be all right," said Aleksi. "I shall walk to the university. It is proper that a poet and poor scholar should walk."

Aleksi seemed to be in high spirits and in a talkative mood.

"I have served my apprenticeship," he informed them all. "I have learned all that the literature of England can teach me. Now I return to become our national poet."

"What will your poetry do for the revolution?" demanded Sonia. "A poet is as useless as a Prince!"

"On the flight from London," said Aleksi, unruffled, "I composed a poem in Essenheimisch. It is an excellent poem."

"Do read it out to us," said Kate.

"Willingly. And since your understanding of the language is not yet perfect, no doubt Prince Rudi will help you by translating."

67

Aleksi drew a piece of paper from his pocket and read out his poem. Rudi, with an expression of long-suffering tolerance, translated it phrase by phrase as he went along.

The subject matter sounded familiar: "I moved at random in an isolation similar to that of a mass of fog drifting at a considerable altitude above mountains and valleys when without warning I observed an assemblage, an army, of yellow flowers on long green stalks. . . ."

Kate and George looked at each other with a wild surmise.

"Why," said Kate, "it's Wordsworth. You know, 'I wandered lonely as a cloud.' "

Aleksi inclined his head. "I acknowledge an influence," he said with dignity. "It is better in Essenheimisch than in English, is it not?"

"It is rubbish," said Sonia. "It is totally irrelevant to the class struggle."

"And where will *you* go now, Sonia?" Kate asked, changing the subject.

"For the moment, I shall go to my father's house."

"Sonia's father," said Rudi, "is not only a count but also one of the richest men in Essenheim."

"That may be so," said Sonia crossly. "It is nothing to me. I did not ask to be begotten by a reactionary plutocrat. I spit on his wealth. But he is my father—he will have to find me a room."

"It seems to me," said Rudi, "that you can probably afford to take a taxi."

11

The day seemed to have been going on forever, and it wasn't by any means over yet. In the Airport Director's shack Kate sat in the usual awkward threesome with Rudi and George. A decrepit taxicab had appeared and been engaged by Sonia. From the customs shack nearby came the sounds of merrymaking—Fritzi and the customs official had evidently uncorked a bottle of Essenheim's finest.

Then there was a crunch of wheels on gravel. Kate and George followed Rudi outside. A stately but elderly Daimler drew up, with a stately but elderly chauffeur at the wheel. There was a coat of arms on the side of the car. From the back jumped a teenage girl, a year or two younger than Kate, wearing a T-shirt and jeans. She flung her arms round Rudi, covered his face with kisses, and then turned to Kate and repeated the performance.

"It's great to meet you!" she declared. "Boy, do I *need* you! It's been desperate here!"

She peered through a long blond fringe at George. "Who's he, Rudi?" she asked.

"He's an English journalist," Rudi said. "He knows everybody."

"*Everybody?*" the girl said. "You mean he knows *famous* people? Like . . . like *deejays?*"

"I'm afraid that's not my line," George said. "Political and diplomatic journalism, that's what I do, mostly."

"Oh."

"I should have introduced you," Rudi said. "Kate and George, this is my sister Anni. My *little* sister."

"Get stuffed, Rudi!" said Anni. And then: "Sit beside me in the car, Kate. I want to talk to you. Oh, it'll be so *good*, talking to someone from London again!"

"Again?" Kate said.

"Yeah. My best friend is from London. Was. That's Betsy. She's the British Consul's daughter. Well, her dad *was* the British Consul here. He got axed in an economy cut. England doesn't have a consul in Essenheim now. Nobody does. I guess we aren't in the world anymore." She sighed deeply.

The Daimler left the airstrip and crossed a bridge over a steep, narrow valley. Houses straggled up and down the slopes, and a river flowed far below. Anni chattered into Kate's ear about the delights of London, and Kate half listened. The car moved off the bridge and down a narrow street, and stopped in front of what was evidently the Ritz-Albany Hotel, for Rudi said, "This is it, George."

George got out, said, "Thanks for the lift. Now take care of yourself, Kate," and waved good-bye as the car rolled away. Kate waved, too, but George had already turned his back on the Daimler.

Next they drove along a tree-lined avenue, across another bridge, and through a gateway, and began a winding ascent to the castle, which loomed gloomily above.

"How'd you like to live in *that* load of architectural crap?" asked Anni.

From the car, Kate could see only that the castle was built from huge blocks of rough stone and that there was a great deal of it. The Daimler drove past a massively forbidding front entrance with great studded wooden doors firmly closed, and then went for some distance round the side of the castle. Near the back was a modest doorway with a light over it; beside the door was a single guard who stood upright but might well have been asleep with his eyes open.

Inside the entrance was a dimly lit stone-flagged passageway, and from it Kate could see, through an open door, a vast echoing kitchen of decidedly medieval aspect. It contained enormous ranges and a great fireplace with a spit that looked big enough to roast a whole ox on; huge copper pans hung on the walls. It looked to Kate as if the kitchen hadn't been used in years, possibly decades. Farther on, the passageway ended at another door; and at the far side of that, looking remarkably modern by contrast, was a fully lit, carpeted hallway of modest size. In this was a desk with a bell on it, which Rudi rang. "My uncle had part of the servants' quarters made into a private apartment," he said. "The rest of the castle's not fit to live in."

"As if this part were," Anni said.

A dark-suited functionary appeared, bowed to Rudi, and said to Kate, "The Prince Laureate sends his apologies for not coming down to greet you in person. He doesn't get around very easily these days. I'll have somebody show you to your room, and then perhaps you'll be kind enough to go and see him before dinner."

Rudi said, "I must have a word with Uncle right away, and then I'll come for you. You'll have plenty of time to change."

"I haven't much to change into," said Kate.

"You have a dress, I suppose? Just a pretty dress is what my uncle likes. He's really very old-fashioned. And, Kate . . ."

"Yes?"

"Don't react to anything he says, however much it surprises you. I'll give you the explanations afterward."

A very young, round-faced maid showed Kate into a bedroom with an extremely high ceiling and a narrow, pointed, deeply recessed window. Kate went over to the window and looked out. The light was beginning to fade, and lamps were coming on; they marked the many layers of the hilly little town. Kate unpacked her suitcase, put out one of the two dresses she'd brought—a floral patterned cotton—and went into the tiny bathroom that opened out of her room. When she came out, freshly showered, Anni was sprawling on the bed.

"Hi, Kate," she said. "I just came visiting." She looked

Kate up and down. "So you're Rudi's new girl friend," she said.

"Oh, am I?" said Kate. "I didn't know that."

"Then why have you come to Essenheim?"

"I thought I was invited by *you*."

Anni looked startled. She said, "Rudi told you that?"

"Yes."

Anni laughed. "Okay, let's make it true. Kate, I invite you to Essenheim. Stay for ages. But don't rely on what Rudi says."

"He's very persuasive," Kate remarked.

"Oh, sure, he's persuasive. Rudi can make anybody do anything. But if I lived in London, you couldn't *pay* me to come to Essenheim."

"Why not?"

"There's nothing to do here. No dances, no concerts, no discos. Just one boy in all of Essenheim who I like, and I can't have anything to do with him because he's only an apprentice. Apart from him, there's nobody my age but peasants and my cousin Friedrich. And Friedrich is the wettest thing since Noah's flood. . . . You know something, Kate? I'm still a virgin."

"Oh?" said Kate.

"I am, truly. Isn't it *disgusting*?"

"How old are you, Anni?"

"Nearly sixteen."

"I wouldn't say it's actually a disgrace to be a virgin at that age," Kate said. "In fact . . ." She had a sudden inspiration and went on, "In fact it's quite fashionable in London. Lots of people think it's *sexy* to be a virgin."

"Oh!" said Anni. The thought was obviously a new

one to her. She was silent for a minute or two, considering it. Then there was a tap at the door and Rudi came in.

"Kate!" he exclaimed. "What a pretty dress. My uncle will be enchanted. . . . He would like to see us both now."

Rudi took Kate down the hall and knocked at a door. The room they entered had obviously been cut out of a much larger one. Apart from a high, triple-arched window and an elaborate turreted clock the size of a telephone booth, the room was done in mid-twentieth-century style. An electric heater occupied a fireplace of multicolored tile. Beside it flickered a television set. Prince Ferdinand Franz Josef the Third, who had been watching it, rose with some effort to his feet.

"Enchanté, mademoiselle," he said.

He was old and decidedly bulky; his eyes were a watery blue and his cheeks heavy. He had side-whiskers and a large drooping mustache. He wore a plum-colored Army uniform, much wider in the waist than in the chest, with a high collar and epaulets.

Kate made a somewhat awkward curtsey.

"So you are the young lady in Rudi's life," the Prince Laureate observed. He seemed to be favorably impressed. "I must congratulate him on his choice. You are quite charming."

Kate tried to think of some way of disclaiming the role assigned to her, but remembered Rudi's request that she not react to anything the Prince said. Fortunately, Prince Ferdinand didn't seem to expect any comment.

"You are of course a commoner?" he said. "That is quite acceptable. We live in a democratic age, do we not? What does your father do, my dear? He has an occupation, I suppose?"

"He's a journalist," Kate said.

"A journalist!" The Prince seemed startled, as if that were rather extreme, even in a democratic age.

"An editor," Rudi added hastily.

"Ah. The editor, perhaps, of the *Times* newspaper?"

"Well, not exactly," said Kate.

"It is not a distinguished calling," the Prince observed. "Still, no doubt some of those who follow it are not wholly ignoble. I myself am but a simple soldier."

The clock in the corner suddenly went into action. A procession of elaborately costumed figures made a circuit of its turreted summit, while a wooden figure of a lightly clad lady played a tune on a built-in dulcimer, the words FLOREAT ESSENHEIM appeared in wildly ornate lettering at a window, and a pair of heraldic birds emerged from hatches, turning their heads from side to side, opening and closing their beaks, and flapping their wings. Then the activity ceased, the window and hatches slammed shut, and with an air of anticlimax the clock struck eight.

"I'm sorry if that startled you," the Prince said to Kate. "I've been meaning to get rid of it for thirty years. It is out of place here, is it not? It was made for my great-grandfather by an excessively loyal craftsman. I don't notice it myself, I'm so used to it. However, it is a reminder. Eight o'clock already. Dr. Stockhausen

75

and his lady are coming to dinner and will arrive any minute. They are invariably prompt." With that he sighed and cast a wistful glance toward the television.

A minute later Dr. and Mrs. Stockhausen were announced. The Prime Minister was an erect, precise-mannered gentleman whose thin hair was strained to the limit to cover his scalp. He had sharp eyes behind rimless spectacles—it seemed to Kate that they were the eyes of an accountant who has spent a lifetime detecting irregularities in the books. His wife was a very large lady in a low-cut dress that displayed impressive expanses of bosom and back.

Dr. Stockhausen bowed stiffly to the old Prince and gave Kate a thin-lipped smile when she was introduced to him. He didn't seem at all pleased to see Rudi.

"I heard only five minutes ago from the Chamberlain that you had arrived, Prince Rudi," he said. "No one had the courtesy to inform me. Am I to understand that you have not deserted us after all, and that it is still your wish to be considered your uncle's heir?"

"If my uncle pleases," Rudi said respectfully. He switched on the smile at its maximum stunning power. It had a devastating effect on Kate and also, she guessed, on Mrs. Stockhausen; but the Prime Minister had clearly developed an immunity. His silence was icy.

At that moment there was a tap at the door and a small, pale, slightly pop-eyed youth sidled into the room. He blinked on seeing Rudi.

"Hello, Friedrich," said Rudi affably.

"H-h-hello, Rudi. I didn't expect to see *you*."

"Well, here I am," Rudi said with a smile. "Kate, my dear, I would like you to meet my cousin Friedrich. Friedrich, this is Kate Milbank, a very dear friend of mine from London."

"H-hello, g-gracious young lady," Friedrich said. Kate had the impression that he was scared to death of her. And she herself was a little alarmed by the emphasis with which Rudi had described her as his "very dear friend."

12

—— ⋖⫷ ⫸⋗ ——

Dinner seemed to Kate to go on for a long time. They had eaten simply but well on their motor trip through France, Switzerland, and Serenia; by contrast, the cuisine of Essenheim seemed simple but dreadful. A thick, appetite-blunting soup was followed by a casserole of beef and then by large slabs of cheesecake; a heavy red wine by a cloying white one. Prince Ferdinand ate steadily, as if conscientiously performing a tiresome royal duty; Mrs. Stockhausen munched in a stately manner. The Prime Minister ate little. He eyed Rudi coldly from time to time and pointedly refrained from talking to him.

The effects of the long day, the heavy food, and the wine combined to make Kate very sleepy, and she found it increasingly difficult to pay attention to the conversation. She did come awake long enough to hear the old Prince say, "Now then! We will want to have a gala of some sort to celebrate the return of the prodigal and to honor his . . . friend, the gracious young lady Kate." At this, Kate glanced in the Prince Laureate's direction and found him beaming at her.

Rudi said, "That is most generous of you, Uncle. Perhaps a reception in the Great Hall? Full dress, of course . . ."

"The cost!" interposed Dr. Stockhausen.

"Bother the cost!" said the old Prince. "I do so little entertaining these days—the people will be complaining that they never see their Prince."

"If I might make a suggestion, Uncle," Rudi said politely, "we could make it a reception in honor of yourself, as well. The anniversary of your coming to the throne is a week from Thursday."

"Good heavens, has that come round again?" The Prince sighed deeply. "How many years is it now? Thirty? And it seems like yesterday!" Then: "Very well. We must invite everyone in the Principality who is of the least importance. Stockhausens, Lackendorfs, Finkels, von Mecklins . . ."

Kate tuned out again. And then finally Rudi was standing behind her chair, ready to pull it out for her. "You are asleep on your feet, dear Kate," he said in a low voice. "Let us bid my uncle good night and I shall conduct you to your room."

The old Prince seemed delighted with the idea that Kate was excusing herself to go to bed, and said something poetic about how a lover might well envy the pillow upon which such a fair head lay. Kate wondered foggily how Aleksi would render the line in Essenheimisch. Then the old Prince said, "And now you may kiss my cheek."

Trying to do what was expected, Kate kissed the Prince Laureate's worn cheek and, for good measure, curtseyed as well. The Prince was still smiling approvingly when Kate and Rudi left the room.

"You have some explaining to do," Kate said to Rudi as he left her at her bedroom door.

"Tomorrow, Kate. That will be soon enough. Tomorrow you shall have your explanation."

Kate was overcome by an enormous yawn. What she wanted right now was to get to bed and sleep.

"All right, tomorrow," she said. "And it had better be good."

In spite of her exhaustion, Kate slept for only a couple of hours. The disturbance to her way of life had upset her system. Just before midnight something jerked her awake and she couldn't get back to sleep. She lay first one way and then another, but her body felt full of itches and fidgets. She got up, had a drink of water, and tried again. Still it didn't work. She'd packed in such a hurry that she hadn't brought anything to read. Finally she decided that a brisk walk through the corridors might make her tired enough to fall asleep again. Besides, it might be instructive—she'd hardly seen anything of the castle. She put on her dressing gown and opened the bedroom door.

From somewhere along the passage she could hear the sound of an early Beatles number being plucked out, uncertainly, with many mistakes, on a guitar. She followed the sound. It came from a room near the end of the passage; the door stood ajar, and Kate peeked in. She saw first that the room seemed to be a sitting room, and then that Friedrich was sitting on a cushion with his back against the wall, frowning with concentration as he tried, slowly and painfully, to find the right notes on the guitar.

Remembering Friedrich's shyness before dinner, and not wanting to startle him, Kate started to withdraw. But Friedrich jerked his head up and cried, "Who's th-there?"

Kate pushed the door open wider and said, "It's only me. I'm sorry if I alarmed you."

Friedrich thrust the guitar aside and scrambled to his feet.

"Don't let me stop you," Kate said hastily.

"You're not s-stopping me. I was going to stop anyway. I d-don't seem able to get it right tonight." He added anxiously, "I c-can play better than this sometimes. I think I'm a b-bit off form."

"Nobody's *always* on top form," said Kate, trying to reassure him.

Friedrich smiled gratefully. There was a brief, awkward silence. Then he said, with some effort, "I h-hope you'll like it in Essenheim."

"I expect I shall," said Kate.

"I'm really g-glad Rudi came back," he went on. "I m-mean, to be the Crown Prince. Now I won't have to do it." He swallowed and wiped his palms on his trousers. "I should hate being Crown Prince or P-prince Laureate. I'd have to m-mix with so many people." He looked desolate at the very thought. "I m-mostly don't know what to say to p-people I don't know," he confided.

As gently as possible, Kate said, "But couldn't the

Prince Laureate name you Crown Prince even though Rudi has come back?"

"Oh, y-yes—but he won't," Friedrich said. "He's always w-wanted Rudi for it. It's only the P-prime Minister who wanted me for the j-job."

"Oh, I see," said Kate.

Another silence followed. Finally Kate smiled and said, "Well, good night. I expect I'll be seeing something of you in the next few days."

"I hope so!" said Friedrich. He blushed, coughed, and then said shyly, "I l-like you, Kate. You have a nice smile."

Kate wandered back down the passage. At the other end of it a window stood open, and she heard a murmur of voices and a low laugh from outside. It was the laugh that caught her attention.

The view from the narrow window was not the same as that from Kate's own room. There was a brief gleam of moonlight, and she saw, below her and not far to the right, a paved and ornamented terrace at the edge of a sheer drop. There were seats on the terrace, and on one of them were a man and a woman, sitting very close together. Kate couldn't see their faces or hear what they were saying, but the voices sounded intimate, and she thought she recognized one of them. When the low laugh came again, she was sure she did.

Rudi.

13

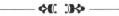

Kate was awakened by the sharp, strident sounds of a raised masculine voice coming from somewhere below her bathroom window. It was broad daylight—after eight o'clock—and a sunny day. She went to the window in her nightgown and looked down into the courtyard below. A squad of some thirty soldiers was drilling under the eye of a massive, erect, and impressive figure, as big as any two of them, with a flat cap, red face, and bristly mustache, and the loudest voice Kate had heard in her life.

Her vocabulary in Essenheimisch didn't include military terms, but there was no mistaking the meaning of his commands: quick march, left turn, right turn, about-face, halt. The squad moved like clockwork, with the exception of one unfortunate in the back row who was forever getting out of step or mistaking the order. He came in for special attention from the commander, who bawled at him repeatedly and eventually separated him from the flock and drilled him mercilessly for five minutes on his own. Kate felt increasingly sorry for him.

There was a tap on her shoulder.

"Hi!" said Anni. "Sleep well?"

"Fine, thanks."

"That's our Army down there."

"All of it?" asked Kate.

"Half of it. There're sixty men altogether. It's enough, I guess. You should hear old Stockhausen complain about the cost. But my uncle won't have it disbanded. He commanded it himself in the war."

"Was Essenheim in the war?"

"Sure it was. We declared war on Germany and Italy two weeks before the end. And Japan, too, but I guess we couldn't get at Japan from here."

"And what did the Army *do*?"

"It was rounded up by a German patrol. Uncle Ferdy wasn't the brightest of commanders. But then Germany lost the war, and Uncle Ferdy got the Essenheim Grand Cross for Gallantry from the Prince Laureate of that time—his father—so he was quite happy about it. In theory he's still the commander, with Rudi as his second. But in practice Schweiner's in charge."

"Schweiner?"

"That's Schweiner down there, drilling them. Colonel Schweiner, promoted from Top Sergeant. Keep clear of him, Kate, he's a bastard."

Kate watched for a few more minutes as the squad marched to and fro. Then the men were halted, and Colonel Schweiner turned to meet someone walking across the courtyard toward him. It was Rudi, also in officer's uniform, looking slim, trim, and extremely handsome.

84

Schweiner brought the Essenheim Army smartly to attention and saluted. Rudi responded with a casual flip of the hand. A few words were spoken, which Kate couldn't hear. Then Schweiner dismissed the squad. The men disappeared round a corner of the castle wall at high speed, as if they were afraid their commander might change his mind. Rudi and Schweiner walked slowly across the courtyard, and then turned and walked back, deep in conversation. Schweiner was twirling a swagger stick. Confidence and self-satisfaction were expressed in every movement he made.

"Come and have some breakfast," said Anni. "Tell me what's happening in London. I keep expecting a letter from my friend Betsy, but it doesn't come."

Kate did her best, realizing that her knowledge of the London that interested Anni was quite limited. Anni, however, did not seem disappointed. "It's great to talk to you," she kept saying over the coffee and rolls. "It's like having an older sister."

"Oh?"

"Not *much* older, of course," Anni said hastily. "I'd hate to be twenty, wouldn't you? I couldn't *bear* to be twenty."

"I expect you will be, someday," said Kate. "It comes to all of us in the end."

"Yeah, I guess so. How disgusting."

Rudi did not appear at breakfast, and all of a sudden Kate felt homesick and low-spirited. She decided she needed to hear an English voice, and went to her room and tried to call George. But the person who answered the phone at the Ritz-Albany Hotel spoke only a dialect of Essenheimisch that Kate found hard to understand. Finally it became clear that the owner of the voice was unable to put George on the line, and Kate hung up feeling frustrated and miserable.

It was then that Rudi tapped at the door and came in. He was still in military uniform. "I apologize for the fancy dress," he said.

"It suits you," said Kate; and it did. Rudi was tall and athletic-looking, and more beautiful than any young man had a right to be. She knew him to be aware of it, and guessed that he traded on it, but it made no difference. She didn't know how to resist charm like that.

Rudi took her in his arms and kissed her slowly, deliberately, meltingly. The suspicion that it was an expert performance, perfected no doubt with a good deal of practice, didn't prevent it from having its effect.

With a huge effort of will Kate rescued herself from the clinch and took a step back.

"Now," she said. "At last. You are going to tell me just why you've brought me to Essenheim and how long you want me to stay. *And* just what you've told your family."

Rudi sighed. "Kate, dear," he said, "I will tell you all. Come with me for a walk in the grounds."

The day was still clear, and becoming warm. They left the modernized corner of the castle by a small back door and strolled across a lawn. Looking behind her, Kate saw that a tower soared skyward from the opposite corner of the castle; it was so high that she had to tip her head back to see to the top.

"You can climb all the way up there," Rudi observed. "It means going up innumerable spirals of stone steps, but the view from the top is marvelous. You can see the whole Principality from up there. Do you wish to go up?"

"Yes, please."

"Very well. One day while you're here I will take you. But not, I think, now."

"No, not now," Kate agreed. "Right now, you're giving me that explanation."

Rudi took a deep breath.

"You know, of course, that I am engaged to be married."

"Yes. You told me."

"To my distant cousin, the Princess Margaretta of Lubenstein. If Germany were to break up into the cluster of Principalities and Dukedoms from which it was assembled, she would be the heiress to a throne and to vast estates. That won't happen, of course. But she *is* the heiress to a famous name and what's left of an enormous fortune. Both of these things cut a great deal of ice with Uncle Ferdy. Especially the fortune."

"He's hard up, isn't he?" said Kate.

"Desperately so. My great-great-grandfather mortgaged the family estates to the hilt to build this castle, of which we use only a tiny corner. Great-grandfather, who succeeded him, didn't help matters by having a weakness for chorus girls and visits to Monte Carlo.

By comparison, Uncle Ferdy is a model of good behavior. He's never had the money to be anything else. His idea of living it up is to sit and watch Serenian television. But he does have one ambition, and that's to retrieve the family fortunes."

"Through your marriage," said Kate.

"Yes."

"I think it's terrible! And what about this poor little girl? Having a husband wished on her while she's practically in the cradle! It's an outrage! She mightn't like you at all when she grows up!"

"Oh, I expect she will," said Rudi confidently. "But that's not quite the point. The point is that, as I told you before, she is just ten years old. There can't be any marriage for another six years."

"Hard luck!" said Kate sardonically.

"Meanwhile, just imagine how boring it is to be Crown Prince of Essenheim, with nothing to do but open bazaars!"

"I'd have thought you could find other things to do if you tried."

"I can, actually. That's what Uncle Ferdy's worried about. He wants me to settle down. With a nice young woman."

"But—" Kate began, and then she stopped short. "Oh!"

"You see, to people of his upbringing and generation, it's the obvious thing to do. If you can't marry for a few years, you take a mistress."

"And you're thinking of that as a job for *me*?" Kate asked incredulously.

"Well . . ." Rudi began. For once he sounded embarrassed. "Well, not exactly."

"Not *exactly*? What do you have in mind, then?"

"I would like you to let my uncle *suppose* you have agreed to such a relationship."

For a moment Kate was startled into silence. Then she asked, "Why choose me? And why should I do any such thing?"

"You see, Kate, suitable young ladies are not easily found. Essenheim itself is a very small world, and the matter is a delicate one. It has long been my uncle's view that I should look outside the country for an—er—associate. He doesn't think it necessary, or even desirable, that she should be an aristocrat. At the same time, he wouldn't wish me to bring a rough, uneducated, or flighty young woman to be virtually his daughter-in-law. A nice young girl of respectable bourgeois parentage would be ideal. . . ."

"And you thought I'd do!" Hurt and humiliated, Kate felt herself to be on the verge of tears.

"It wasn't like that, Kate. Believe me, I like you too much to urge an unwelcome role upon you. But please let me continue. How old do you suppose my uncle to be?"

"I don't know. I haven't thought about it." Kate was struggling to calm herself.

"He is seventy-six. He has been Prince Laureate of Essenheim for thirty years. His health isn't good; he's overweight and he has trouble with his back and with his breathing. Above all, Kate, he is weary. He has had enough of being Prince Laureate. He would like to retire—that is, to abdicate. To abdicate in my favor."

"Why doesn't he, then?" Kate asked. "It would give you something to do."

"Why doesn't he? Partly because of Dr. Stockhausen's opposition. As you know, Dr. Stockhausen doesn't approve of me."

"But your uncle's an absolute ruler. Surely he can just *sack* Dr. Stockhausen! The kidnap attempt would be a good reason."

"I shan't say anything about the kidnap attempt. There wouldn't be any point. Dr. Stockhausen would deny all knowledge of it. And sacking him is more easily said than done. He has his hands on so many of the levers. Uncle Ferdy did sack him once, but he ignored being sacked, and eventually Uncle thought better of it. However, it's not only Dr. Stockhausen. The fact is that Uncle himself doesn't quite trust me. He *likes* me, but he doesn't *trust* me."

"I can understand that," said Kate.

"The obvious time for him to abdicate would be when I marry. But that's six years away. He'll be eighty-two, if he's still alive. He doesn't want to wait that long. So . . ."

He hesitated, then went on, "So I made a bargain with my uncle. If I would settle down with a suitable young woman, he would abdicate right away. And as you know, Kate, I do wish to become Prince Laureate." He added hastily, "It's not that I care about the title, of course. I want to be Prince Laureate so that I can bring progress and modern ideas to my country."

Kate stared at him bleakly. Rudi took her hand and

said, "I am asking for your help, Kate."

"My *help*! I'd say you were asking for something a little more than that!"

"But I'm not," Rudi said earnestly. "I promise you that I shan't insist on any . . . marital rights, so to speak. You will have your own room; I shall not set foot in it uninvited. As soon as my accession is an accomplished fact you can go back to London, if you want."

Kate said, "You just need me so you can convince your uncle that you're a safe, reliable fellow. A married man in all but name."

Rudi beamed. "Yes, you understand perfectly. And I do not think you would have to pose as my consort for very long. You see, this reception next Thursday is the perfect time for my uncle to announce his abdication. Everyone who is anyone in Essenheim will be there—the entire aristocracy and professional hierarchy. Young Moritz from the radio station and old Beyer who owns the Essenheim newspaper will also attend, and so will your friend George from the British press. If my uncle names me Prince Laureate in front of such an assemblage, Dr. Stockhausen will be helpless—no argument will be possible. I shall be Prince Laureate! And although I intend that democracy will follow, I shall for the moment be the absolute ruler. If Stockhausen objects, I can have him thrown into jail!"

Rudi was clearly delighted with himself. He added, "If you wished to stay on after I became Prince Laureate, you would be very welcome, not least by me. But I would not try to hold you."

Kate had a strong impulse to slap his face.

"You want me to deceive that poor old man!" she cried. "And *you've* been deceiving *me*! This was supposed to be 'just a holiday' for me—do you remember saying that? You said it to my father! Do you think it's any holiday for me to have you—to . . ." She turned away abruptly so that Rudi couldn't see how hurt she was. Then, in a low voice, she continued, "You never cared about me at all. It was my father you wanted to meet in the first place, because of his job—not me. I was just stupid enough to think you might really like me."

"Kate, dear," Rudi said, sounding abashed, "I *did* like you, from the beginning. You must believe me. I like you very much. Why else would I seek you out and bring you to Essenheim?"

"Because you hadn't anyone better at the time, I expect! Well, I've told you, Rudi, I won't have anything to do with this scheme. I absolutely refuse. I shall tell your uncle the truth!"

"My poor uncle," Rudi said sadly. "You could make him so happy if you wished. The deception would be so unimportant, the equivalent of a small white lie, and his relief on abdicating would be so great. He has waited so long for an excuse." He sighed. "You are hard, Kate. I didn't think you would be so hard."

"You know what, Rudi?" said Kate. "You're the most devious person I've ever met! And I'm beginning to think you're also the biggest phony!"

Rudi looked at her with appealing brown eyes. He seemed hurt. Suddenly Kate wanted to run her hand through his hair. She couldn't believe she'd just said he was a phony. Part of her thought that he was, but another part of her was saying that she must be misjudging him, that he was in a difficult position, and that his actions were probably all for the best.

Rudi must have seen that she was wavering, for he said, "I beg you to reconsider, Kate. For my uncle's sake . . . and for mine as well."

Kate said nothing.

"Please think about it," Rudi said. "Just think about it, that's all I ask."

14

———— ❖❉( )❉❖ ————

"Kate, my dear," said the Prince Laureate after lunch, "come and talk to me for a few minutes."

Kate followed him into his little private salon. The television set was on. Prince Ferdinand hobbled to it and switched it off. "It is my drug," he said. "Keep me off it for a while."

Kate helped him into his armchair and seated herself on a stool close by. He's a nice, harmless old man, she thought; harmless and lonely.

He looked at her with evident approval. "Now that I see you by daylight," he said, "I like you even more. Perhaps Rudi has good taste after all. When he said he had brought a lady home, I must admit that I wondered what sort of a lady it might be. But you, my dear, an unspoiled English girl of ordinary family . . ."

The Prince smiled. There was a hint of Rudi in his smile, but it was a sweeter smile, and in an odd way more innocent. "You will be a charming companion for Rudi. It's a pity you're a commoner, my dear, and without fortune. If your origins were suitable, I should not in the least mind Rudi's marrying you. But that, of course, cannot be. You understand, I am sure."

"Oh, yes," said Kate dryly.

"The only thing that worries me," the Prince Laureate said, "is that you may be too good for Rudi."

Kate stared.

"Don't look so surprised," he said. "I am fond of my nephew. It is my dearest wish that he should succeed me. But he's a little wild, a little unreliable. He gets his way with people rather too easily, and has been known to let them down. I should not wish that to happen to you."

"I don't think it will," said Kate with all the firmness she could muster.

"You have spirit, my dear!" The Prince smiled again. "That's good, that's good. . . . And Rudi says you have even learned our language."

Kate smiled and said carefully in Essenheimisch, "A little, gallant Highness. I took lessons in London."

"Bravo!" said the Prince, beaming. "At the reception next Thursday you must greet the guests in Essenheimisch. Then you will be—as you would say—a big hit. Of course," he added, "such a delightful young lady as yourself would be a big hit in any event."

"Thank you," Kate said faintly. She was beginning to feel a bit embarrassed by all the compliments the old Prince was paying her.

"Rudi has been seeing to your happiness, I trust?" he now asked rather sternly. "I am an old man and live simply, yet I think I know what young ladies require. There are flowers in your room? Scented soap? Enough towels? The maid seems to you discreet? I believe we have some pink silk cushions in storage somewhere. . . ."

Now Kate did feel embarrassed. Fortunately, Anni bounced into the room just then. "I want the two good horses this afternoon!" she declared. "I want Kate to ride with me. You do ride, don't you, Kate?"

"Not really," said Kate. She'd once had a few lessons, but she hadn't ridden much.

"Of course you do!" Anni said. "And it's a lovely afternoon. We'll take a ride up into the valley."

"Just the thing, my dear," said the Prince approvingly; and, to Kate: "That will put some color in your cheeks. I mustn't keep you sitting here talking to an old man."

Kate rose. She thought of curtseying, but then changed her mind and kissed the old Prince's cheek before going out with Anni.

"You look pleased with yourself, Rudi," Anni remarked. "What have you been up to while we were riding?"

"None of your business," said Rudi cheerfully. "But I'm taking you out to dinner, both of you."

"Me as well?" Anni sounded surprised.

"Yes, you as well."

"Why do I get to come? Has Uncle Ferdy insisted on a chaperone?"

"You could be right."

"I bet I *am* right." Anni turned to Kate. "In Uncle Ferdy's world there are two kinds of girls, good girls and bad girls. Good girls get chaperoned. You count as a good girl, Kate. I guess it wouldn't do for you to be seen in public alone with Rudi. Not just yet, anyway."

"Uncle Ferdy lives in the past," said Rudi. "Except for the television. He'll be glad to have us out of the way this evening, so he can have a quiet supper in front of it."

Rudi drove the two girls through the cobbled streets and squares of Essenheim, which were lined with small shops, color-washed houses, and little pavement cafés; and then through the country to the Spitzhof, an extremely smart and expensive-looking restaurant perched on a crag overlooking the Esel River. The manager greeted Rudi with a casual "Evening, Highness"; and the barman inquired, "The usual, Highness?" on serving drinks before dinner. Kate experimented with a special Essenheim drink that tasted like toothpaste-flavored kerosene, and was relieved to replace it with mineral water. The meal that followed, however, was far above the standard at the castle.

After dinner Anni slipped away to talk to someone she knew. She had hardly left the table when a stranger approached. He was a short man in late middle age, plump in a sleek, shiny way, as if he owed it to years of eating excellent food. His face was pink and round, without a wrinkle; his eyes were smallish, shrewd, and

97

blue; his hair blond but graying, and very short. His suit was impeccably cut and obviously expensive. He clicked his heels when Rudi introduced him to Kate as Herr Finkel.

"Delighted, gracious young lady," he said, and bowed.

"Herr Finkel has been closely associated with my family for many years," Rudi said.

"I have indeed had that honor," said Herr Finkel.

At Rudi's invitation, he took the chair that Anni had left. Gravely, in excellent English, he interrogated Kate about her family, her interests and occupations, her work at school, her intentions for the future. He listened with courteous interest to all she said. Kate, like many other people, found herself a fascinating topic; when encouraged she was very willing to hold forth. So for a quarter of an hour she enjoyed herself, talking ever more freely. Then suddenly she became aware of a calculating mind behind Herr Finkel's shrewd eyes and realized that he'd been interviewing her, almost like a prospective employer. She broke off in midsentence and said, "I'm surprised that you're so interested, Herr Finkel."

"*Naturally* I am interested in a close friend of his Highness," said Herr Finkel. "It has been a great pleasure to meet you, Miss Milbank." He got up to go. "I should be happy if his Highness found it possible to bring you for a meal at my home sometime soon."

Kate said nothing to that. Rudi said noncommittally, "That would be very pleasant."

Herr Finkel said, "Your servant, Highness. Your servant, gracious young lady," clicked his heels again, and withdrew.

Anni was still talking animatedly with a party of youngish people two or three tables away. Rudi leaned over and said in a low voice, "Well? Have you decided what you're going to do?"

"Do?" said Kate. "Oh. No, I—I haven't had much time to think." She avoided Rudi's eyes. She knew that she had already decided to go along with his scheme, and told herself she was doing it for Prince Ferdinand's sake—he was so old, and so nice, and if he wanted to abdicate, surely it would be cruel to prevent him from doing so. But a corner of her mind insisted that she was actually giving in to Rudi's charms, and that it might be a very bad idea to let him know it. She added feebly, "It's a rather complicated moral question."

Rudi favored her with a tender smile. "If only you would trust me, dearest Kate," he said.

"I wouldn't trust him *too* much, if I were you," said Anni cheerfully, returning to the table. "What's he talking about, Kate?"

"Nothing that concerns you!" Rudi said in an elder-brother tone of voice.

"I noticed you were chatting to the paymaster," Anni remarked.

"The paymaster?" Kate said.

"That was old Finkel, wasn't it? The richest man in Essenheim. Owns this restaurant, among much else. He owns *us*, lock, stock, and barrel. Our great-great-grandfather borrowed from Finkel's grandfather to build the castle, and since that time we've never been

99

out of debt to the Finkels. Right, Rudi?"

"That's correct," Rudi said coldly.

"Now if we're talking about trusting," Anni said, "*there's* a man not to trust. I'd trust old Finkel about as far as I can throw a grand piano. With one hand."

15

Kate wasn't one of those people who worry their lives away. She woke up the next morning feeling cheerful and optimistic. She had decided that she didn't at all mind staying in Essenheim until after next week's reception, and that it would be fun to see the installation of Rudi as Prince Laureate and the discomfiture of starchy old Dr. Stockhausen. In the meantime, she was in Essenheim on holiday, and she meant to make the most of it.

That day was, in fact, the beginning of a pleasant interlude. The weather in Essenheim was clear and warm but not oppressively hot. Rudi was attentive to her; he had a small and not new but decidedly zippy sports car, and he drove Kate round most of the narrow winding roads of the Principality. The royal launch *Lorelei* was cleaned up and serviced, and the Royal Essenheim Navy, consisting of Commander Himmelwein and Able Riverman Flusswasser, took Rudi, Anni, Kate, Friedrich, and a couple of other royal cousins on a languorous all-day river trip past the villages and vineyards that lined the banks of the Esel. Children

101

ran down to the water's edge to wave and shout, "Hello, Highnesses," and Kate felt rather like royalty herself.

She realized that the Prince Laureate and Anni were becoming increasingly fond of her. The old Prince would call her in for little chats, and always paid her the high compliment of turning off the television set. Anni took her out riding, or to swim in a pool that belonged to one of the cousins, and informed Kate of her tastes in music, movies, and pop stars. They discovered one afternoon that they were the same dress size.

"Oh, thank goodness!" said Kate. "I didn't bring anything suitable for the reception, you know. Could you lend me a dress, Anni?"

"Of course. Help yourself," said Anni.

Kate riffled through the quantities of dresses in Anni's wardrobe. There were dozens of silk and taffeta confections in bright colors, all covered with frills, sashes, lace, and sequins.

"Aren't they *terrible?*" said Anni gloomily. "I have to use the court dressmaker. Same one as in my granny's day, and she was old-fashioned then. What I wouldn't give for one hour's shopping in London!"

"This one's okay," said Kate at last. She had found a totally plain, off-the-shoulder, rather clinging black silk thing. "It's very nice, in fact."

"It's a nightgown!" said Anni.

"Just the same, I shall wear it," declared Kate, standing in front of the mirror and holding the black nightgown against herself.

"Well, if you're wearing that, I shall wear *this*," said Anni, producing a similar nightgown in white. "Do you think we dare?"

"Of course we do!" said Kate.

On alternate evenings Kate phoned her father and told him what she'd been doing; she never had any difficulty getting through, and Edward was glad to hear that she was having a good time. The one thing that surprised him, and surprised Kate too when she came to think about it, was that she didn't see or hear anything of George. He didn't present himself at the castle, and Kate wasn't able to reach him by phone—he was never available, and no one ever knew where he was. But finally, after a week, Kate called the hotel at a time when George himself answered the phone.

"Well, Kate, how nice to hear from you," George said rather sardonically.

"You might have called *me*," Kate replied. "But I suppose you've just been *too* busy working on your stories."

It turned out that George had tried to call Kate frequently; she protested that no one had ever told her of his calls. And no one at the Ritz-Albany had told George of Kate's calls to him, either.

"Very fishy," said George. "I'm beginning to feel as if I'm in a spy novel. There's a fellow who I think is watching me. I keep seeing him across the street or waiting outside, and I'm sure that when I go out he follows."

103

"What sort of a fellow?" Kate asked.

"A big blond man with cropped hair and the look of a bouncer."

It sounded rather like Karl, whom Kate had seen in London. "I'll ask Rudi about it," she said.

"Oh, Rudi . . ." said George, without enthusiasm. Then he added unwillingly, as if professional need were conquering personal reluctance, "I suppose I ought to have a talk with Rudi one of these days, if I could do it without attracting attention."

"I'll ask him about that, too," said Kate. And on Sunday morning she mentioned George to Rudi.

"Oh, George," Rudi said coldly. "His problems are none of my affair, Kate. He is, after all, a foreigner and a journalist."

"Well, I'm a foreigner, too," Kate pointed out.

"That is different," Rudi said with a thin smile. "I like you. I do not much like George."

Kate wondered for a wild, delicious moment if Rudi and George were jealous of each other on account of her, but she wasn't quite vain enough to believe it.

Later in the day Rudi seemed to have changed his attitude.

"I've arranged for George to come and see me tomorrow morning," he told Kate. "I'm giving him an interview on the understanding that he won't publish anything until after the reception on Thursday. Then, when I've taken over, he can put the story of Uncle Ferdy's abdication through to London with the interview as background. That should be quite a scoop for him *and* your father, shouldn't it?" He smiled the winning smile. "And I've gotten old Stockhausen to take Karl off George's tail," he added.

"That's more than you could do for yourself, isn't it?" asked Kate in some surprise.

"There was an element of bluff," Rudi said. "As I told you, if I were to tell my uncle about the kidnap attempt, Dr. Stockhausen would deny all knowledge. But he would rather not *have* to deny it. That gave me just enough leverage to get Karl removed." Rudi frowned. "All the same, Karl's activities are a sign that Dr. Stockhausen is keeping his eyes and ears open. He's a wily old bird, and if he got to know of our plans, there's no telling what he might do."

"I shan't tell anyone," Kate assured him.

"Anyway," Rudi said, "George won't be able to complain that I'm not being helpful. And as I have a busy day tomorrow, I've suggested that after the interview he might like to take you out with him. I've fixed up a visit to the university, which will be useful for George and interesting for you. You can meet my friend Klaus Klappdorf there."

"Well," said George next morning. "So there you are."

"Yes," said Kate. "So here I am."

There was a pause.

"It's nice to see you," said George.

"It's nice to see *you*," said Kate, a little less than wholeheartedly. She wasn't particularly thrilled at the thought of an outing with George.

"I've just been talking to Prince Rudi," George said.

"I know," Kate replied. And after that there seemed to be nothing to do but get into George's rented car and head for the university.

"Rudi said the university's in the old pickle factory," George told Kate. "He said we can't miss it, and he promised he'd ask his friend Klaus Something-or-other to look out for us."

In fact they couldn't and didn't miss the old pickle factory. It was all in red brick, and was the biggest building Kate had seen in Essenheim apart from the castle. The legend FINKEL'S PICKLES had been built into the facade with different-colored bricks, but a painted sign over the main gateway now said UNIVER-SITY OF ESSENHEIM.

They were barely inside the yard when they were stopped by a young man and a girl who planted themselves firmly in front of the car.

"Where are you going?" the young man asked in aggressive Essenheimisch.

"Into the university," George said. And, when neither of them moved: "May we come through?"

"What do you want to come through for? What are you doing here?"

"Press," said George. "We have an appointment."

"We don't like the press."

"Spies!" hissed the girl.

"If I were you," the young man said to George, "I'd back out through that gate and head back into town. Quickly."

Kate and George looked at each other helplessly.

But then there was a cry of "Hello, there! Hello!" and a tall, thin man with a ginger beard came bustling across the yard. "It's all right, people," he said to the girl and young man, and the two of them slipped away as suddenly as they had appeared.

"Allow me to introduce myself," the ginger-bearded man said. "I am Klaus Klappdorf, Dean of the Faculty of Arts, Sciences, and Other Studies. Welcome to the University of Essenheim!" He reached through the open window of the car and pumped George's hand, adding, "Rudi told me you were on your way. Why don't you park over there, and I will give you the grand tour."

When they had parked and gotten out of the car, Klaus Klappdorf pumped George's hand again and said, "You will be George. And you, gracious young lady," he said with a bow, "you will be Kate."

He escorted them up the front steps and through the entrance of the former pickle factory.

"I hope you were not alarmed by the students who stopped your car," he went on. "We encourage them to display a little healthy aggression. Here at the university we feel that a militant student is a well-adjusted student."

A clutch of young people in dirty jeans, most with uncombed hair, emerged from a doorway they were passing. Beside the doorway was a placard that read PASSIVE RESISTANCE 102.

"Is passive resistance taught as a course for credit?" asked George, startled.

"To be sure!" Klaus said happily. "As you may know,

this university was founded only twelve years ago, when Herr Finkel decided that pickles were no longer a profitable business. When the university opened, we felt that we ought to have our own specialty, something this university could become known for. Something that wasn't done elsewhere. And we hit upon Studentship Studies."

George looked up at Klaus with a dubious expression. Klaus, unaware of it, went on, "The young people who come to the University of Essenheim are students for four of the most formative years of their lives. What ought they to be studying? The answer is obvious, isn't it? They should be studying the thing that most concerns them, namely, being a student. So"—he cleared his throat—"so we have established Studentship Studies, in the context of the interpersonal and transsocietal relationship structure that we seek to encourage through a meaningful, ongoing dialogue between the new generation and the world that surrounds it. The world of today."

George wrote this down in his notebook and said dryly, "I see."

Kate, hoping to help George out, asked, "What other classes are there besides passive resistance?"

"The curriculum is comprehensive," Klaus said earnestly. "All students are trained not only in passive resistance, but in all other riot tactics. Of course," he said apologetically, "we don't have many riots in Essenheim, but some students go on to foreign capitals for graduate study. The advanced students take Revolu-

108

tionary Tactics and Rhetoric with Ms. Sonia Zackendorf, our Deputy Dean of Arts, Sciences, and Other Studies. And, to give further breadth, we have just appointed a poet-in-residence, a brilliant young man called Aleksi Wandervogel."

"We've met Aleksi and Sonia," said Kate.

"I'm afraid you won't see them here today. They are in a slight difficulty as a result of the bourgeois prejudices of a local judge."

George expressed interest in this situation, but Klaus went on hurriedly, "And of course there is the schlagfuss team, coached by Herr Schwarz. Schlagfuss is our national sport. I believe there is a practice match going on right now. Let me take you to have a look at it."

At first sight, the schlagfuss field looked like an ordinary soccer field. On it two teams of burly male students opposed each other in a game that appeared to be a mixture of soccer, hockey, and street warfare. Players with stout sticks aimed blows indiscriminately at a ball and at any accessible parts of their opponents' bodies. Reserves waited on the sidelines, ready to take the places of any who might be carried off injured.

"Schlagfuss is not a game for the weak," Klaus observed with satisfaction.

"There seems to be some meaningful ongoing dialogue," said George as two players, shouting abuse and taking swipes at each other with their sticks, were separated by the referee at some risk to his own life and limb.

109

"It is good training," said Klaus. "One of these days it may turn out to be very useful."

"Now for the Mayor," said George as they drove away from the University of Essenheim.

"I hadn't even realized there *was* a Mayor," Kate said. "Is he very important?"

"I don't think he seems very important to the powers that be," said George. "But he's the only representative of the ordinary people, so I feel I ought to see him."

Essenheim Town Hall was a modest, squarish stone building behind the marketplace. Mayor Feldbach received them instantly. He was a shirt-sleeved, clean-shaven man in late middle age. His thick dark hair was graying, his eyes were sharp, his expression was shrewd if a little worried. His physique was powerful, and he looked as if he could defend himself, given half a chance. Maybe he had once been a schlagfuss player.

"It's not often that I see any foreign press," he remarked. "Does the Prime Minister know you've come to see me?"

"I don't know," said George frankly. "I thought the Prime Minister didn't even know I was in the country. Then I realized the other day that someone was following me. But there's no sign of him today."

"There are others in Essenheim besides the Prime Minister who might be very interested in your presence here," the Mayor told George.

"Oh? Who?"

"Well, there's Colonel Schweiner, for one. His ambitions rise far above the command of a little Army like ours. And although the force he controls must seem derisory to you, it could be formidable in our small, peaceable country."

Kate shuddered. She hadn't liked the look of Colonel Schweiner at all.

"And there's another power in the land," the Mayor went on. "Come to the window. Look. You see the big white house on the hillside over there?"

"A mansion!" said George. "Is that a private home?"

"It is indeed. It has thirty-nine rooms."

"The owner must be rich."

"He *is* rich. Very rich."

"I can guess who it is!" Kate exclaimed. "Herr Finkel!"

"You are right," said the Mayor. He sighed.

"It sounds as if you don't like him," observed George.

"I will be frank with you," said the Mayor. "So far as the people of Essenheim are concerned, Herr Finkel is the burden we have to bear. I stand up to him as best I can, but it is difficult. He would have me in the bargain basement—that is to say, the castle dungeons—if he could."

"Tell me why he's such a burden," George said.

"He owns most of the Principality. We are peasants and winegrowers and a few shopkeepers. In hard times, Herr Finkel has advanced money to almost everyone. Indeed, he is the only source of money in the Principality. He owns the bank, he owns the radio station, he owns the only large store in the town, he owns the Spitzhof Restaurant."

111

"Princess Anni says he almost owns the castle," said Kate.

"So I believe. Well, we ordinary folk don't care much what happens at the castle, so long as it leaves us in peace. But we're squeezed by Herr Finkel. He owns the winery, you know. The growers used to press their grapes in their own cellars, but now they have to send them to Herr Finkel for pressing."

"And if they don't?"

"He has his strong-arm men. Unpleasant things happen to those who resist him. I can defend myself better than most, but even I have been beaten up in my time. I knew it was Herr Finkel's men, but I couldn't prove it."

"If Rudi succeeds the present Prince," said Kate, wishing she was free to tell the Mayor that the succession would be almost immediate, "surely he'll stop all that kind of thing."

"Perhaps," said the Mayor doubtfully. "He would not find it easy to steer a course between those two, Schweiner and Finkel."

"I have the impression," said George, "that Prince Rudi is steering a very complicated course already."

16

—————— ❖◀❪ ❫▶❖ ——————

On Tuesday morning, with the weather still sunny, Kate went out early by herself and walked about the castle grounds. At length she came to a little paved terrace looking out over the deep gorge that divided the town of Essenheim. She leaned over a white-painted wrought-iron railing and studied the morning scene. On the river far below, the boats looked like tiny toys. Across the gorge were the roofs of the Low Town and, standing high above them, the great white mansion of Herr Finkel.

Essenheim seemed peaceful and lovely this morning. Kate found herself daydreaming. She lived here; the terrace was hers, and she would have her coffee and rolls brought to her here on such a day as this. Rudi would sit opposite . . .

"Oh, come off it, Kate!" she said to herself aloud, disgustedly, and she set off back toward the castle. As she approached the rear courtyard she heard staccato commands and the movement of boots on gravel disturbing the morning peace. It sounded like Colonel Schweiner drilling his men. But when she rounded the corner, Kate saw that only one unfortunate soldier was being drilled. It was the gangling fellow who'd been getting everything wrong the other day. With a heavy pack on his back he was racing at the double, back and forth, left turning, right turning, and about-facing as Schweiner roared orders at him. His face was red with effort and pouring with sweat, and his heavy panting could be heard in the brief intervals between the commands. Schweiner, intent on the drill, didn't notice Kate at first, and she was horrified by the look of gloating enjoyment on his face.

When Schweiner did notice her, his face straightened instantly and he shouted a "Halt" order. The soldier, in a state of near collapse, stood saggingly at attention. He was young, with a blank round face and frightened eyes.

"To your quarters, dismissed!" Schweiner snapped; and as the young soldier tottered away the Colonel, formerly Top Sergeant, turned with an ingratiating smile to Kate.

"Punishment drill, gracious young lady," he explained, wiping sweat from his own beefy face.

Kate didn't feel it was up to her to ask what the young man's crime had been, but her expression must have shown that she was disturbed, for Schweiner added, "It doesn't do them any harm, a good workout. These poor physical specimens *need* hard exercise. He'll live to thank me for it."

Now he looked Kate up and down in considerable detail, and seemed to like what he saw. Kate, unused to being surveyed in such a way, recalled Rudi's early

114

remark about Essenheim standards of feminine beauty. Perhaps, she thought, here in Essenheim she was glamorous. But that didn't save her from feeling deeply repelled by Colonel Schweiner's evident interest. She tried to move on, but the Colonel detained her by dropping a hefty paw on her arm.

"Allow me, gracious young lady," he said, "to welcome you to Essenheim in the name of the Army."

"Thank you," Kate said faintly, and she tried to detach herself. The Colonel's grip tightened.

"It is a great pleasure to us all," he said, "to have someone so young and beautiful in the castle."

Kate made no response. Colonel Schweiner perceived that his remarks were not being warmly received. "You must forgive me, gracious young lady," he said, "if I seem overfamiliar. I am, alas, a widower. I have a daughter of about your own age, and paternal feelings come naturally to me."

It seemed to Kate that the look in his eye was not at all paternal. And he didn't show any fatherly delight when, at that moment, a young woman came into the courtyard and addressed him as "Papa."

"This is my daughter, Elsa, gracious young lady," he said stiffly. And to Elsa he said, "You have the honor of meeting Prince Rudi's friend, of whom we have heard so much."

Kate thought that the description of Elsa as "about her own age" was not quite accurate—she looked to be about thirty. She was remarkably homely, with a long thin nose, small, close-set eyes, and an angular figure.

The ingratiating smile returned to the Colonel's face. "I hope I am not presumptuous," he said, "but I would find it pleasant if you two young ladies could become friends, great friends. I am sure you have much in common."

Kate smiled and said, "Hi!" but was startled by the look of sheer hostility that flashed from Elsa's eyes. There was an almost audible silence. The smirk froze on the Colonel's face. And then Rudi appeared round the corner. Instantly a moony look came over Elsa's face, and as Rudi came closer she curtseyed deeply. And the cause of her resentment was clear to Kate: Elsa was in love with Rudi. Kate didn't think, somehow, that Elsa had much chance of attracting him, but that, of course, wouldn't prevent her from suffering the pangs of love. And jealousy.

Colonel Schweiner snapped to attention and saluted. Rudi responded with his casual flip of the hand, and ignored Elsa altogether. "Ah, there you are, Kate," he said. "Come and have some breakfast."

Both Schweiners stood stock-still as Rudi bore Kate away. She didn't look round, but she could feel the two pairs of eyes still on her.

"We will go," said Rudi at breakfast, "down to old Beyer's printing shop, to collect the invitations for the reception. I must go for them myself, to be sure he's got them right. And it may interest you to see our news sheet, the *Essenheim Free Press*, which Beyer owns. It appears twice a week, and one of the editions will be going to press just about now. I'm afraid it's not quite like the *Daily Intelligence*."

Herr Beyer's printing shop was in the market square, a few doors away from the town hall. It smelled of ink and hot metal. Herr Beyer himself was setting head lines by hand in a compositor's stick when they arrived. His apprentice sat at the keyboard of an ancient, stuttering typesetting machine, painfully picking out the letters. The front page of the *Essenheim Free Press* lay, partly assembled in metal, on a table in the center of the floor.

"That hole in the page is for the main story, Highness," said Herr Beyer. He was a small, thin, wizened man wearing an exceedingly dirty once-white apron. "It's about the reception on Thursday, of course. And about your visit, gracious young lady."

"Fame at last," said Kate. As a journalist's daughter, she wasn't all that excited.

The apprentice called in Essenheimisch from his keyboard, "How do you spell 'castle,' master?"

Herr Beyer tut-tutted and told him. "Half illiterate, Highness, that's what he is," he complained to Rudi. "If I want something done properly I have to do it myself."

"Then I hope you did the invitations yourself," Rudi said.

"Of course, Highness," said Herr Beyer. He wiped his hands on his apron—though it was hard to see how either hands or apron could be improved by this operation—and led the way to a corner of the printing shop,

117

where a pile of large, handsome, deckle-edged cards was stacked. Herr Beyer picked up the top one, stamping it with a big black thumbprint.

"It's all right, Highness," he observed, noticing Rudi's eyes on this. "I've printed plenty. A few spoils are allowed for." .

The cards were printed in Gothic type. They read:

His Illustrious Highness,
Prince Ferdinand Franz Josef 111,
Prince Laureate of Essenheim,
Duke of Teufelwald,
Count of the Two Rivers,
Baron Schatztal,
Field Marshal, Admiral of the Fleet,
Commodore of the
Royal Essenheim Air Force...

"I didn't know Essenheim had an Air Force," Kate said to Rudi.

"You didn't look on the other side of the plane we flew in, did you?" said Rudi. "It says 'Royal Essenheim Airways' on one side and 'Royal Essenheim Air Force' on the other."

"Oh," said Kate, and she went on reading:

presents his humble compliments to

_____

_____

and begs to request the pleasure of his/her company at
A Grand Reception
to celebrate the 30th anniversary of the Prince

118

Laureate's accession to the throne; to welcome the
Prince Rudolf Wilhelm on his return to the
Principality; and further to celebrate the visit to
Essenheim of the Lady Katherine of Hammersmith.

R.S.V.P.

Kate stared at the last item. "Who on earth," she
asked, "is the Lady Katherine of Hammersmith? I live
in Hammersmith myself and I've never heard of her."

"It's you," said Rudi. "Uncle thought it sounded better, and would ensure that the royal relatives treat
you with proper respect. Some of them are apt to be
a bit high and mighty with mere commoners."

"Oh."

"Well, are you happy with them, Highness?" Herr
Beyer asked.

"Very nice," said Rudi, "Now what about some enve-
lopes to put them in?" While he and Herr Beyer dis-
cussed this question, Kate wandered round the printing
shop, examining the presses and the cases of type.
Everything looked extremely old; the typesetting
machine, clanking and chattering away in a corner,
was the most modern feature. She paused to watch
the apprentice at work. He was a curly-haired lad with
a freckled nose and an open, innocent expression.

"Gracious young lady!" he whispered, and then cast
a glance across the room at his master and pressed
two or three keys by way of keeping his machine at
work. "Gracious young lady!"

Kate signified that she was listening.

"You're at the castle, gracious young lady?"

119

Kate nodded.

"Do you see the . . . the Princess Anni?"

"Every day," said Kate.

"Isn't she . . . oh, isn't she . . . isn't she *great*?" The lad blushed crimson and rattled out a machine-gun burst of typesetting.

"There, I got it full of mistakes," he said. "I'm sorry, gracious young lady, I hadn't any right. I just couldn't help myself. I *had* to speak to somebody who speaks to Princess Anni."

"Hey, Hansi, what's going on over there?" called Herr Beyer from the other end of the room.

"I just asked the gracious young lady how to spell 'reception,' " said Hansi.

"You've no business asking the gracious young lady anything!" said Herr Beyer crossly. "If you want to know how to spell 'reception,' you ask me. You ought to know how to spell it anyway. I beg your pardon, gracious young lady. I'm afraid he's a simpleton."

Hansi looked down, abashed. Kate thought he was rather nice, and not a simpleton at all. She wondered if he was the boy whom Anni liked but couldn't have anything to do with because he was only an apprentice.

"Now," Rudi said as they got back into his car, "I must take you to the radio station. They'd like you to go on the air for a few minutes, just to say hello. After that there won't be anything more to do. You can relax until the reception. And then, if you *must*, you can go home." He sighed and flicked a glance at her from under his long eyelashes. "I shall have to begin my

120

reign without you," he observed sadly.

"I'll have served my purpose, won't I?" Kate said with such sharpness as she could muster.

"Oh, Kate, Kate!" said Rudi. He took her hand and held it intermittently all the way to the radio station, which was on the southern heights a little way out of town.

The facade of the station was ultramodern and neon lit; plate-glass doors slid apart and the lobby was carpeted. "It belongs to Herr Finkel," Rudi said, as if this explained everything. But obviously funds had not been unlimited. Beyond the lobby, Radio Essenheim dwindled rapidly to a couple of small rooms and a single studio. The station director, who was waiting for them, said defensively, "It is all due for rebuilding on a larger scale."

Then Kate found herself in the studio, seated opposite a bespectacled young man in a multicolored shirt— the announcer. He offered her a welcoming grimace. A pop record which had figured in the charts some eighteen months ago was just coming to an end. The announcer followed it with some extremely fast talking, in tones of mixed delight and astonishment, about the virtues of a potion that cured rheumatism, headaches, diseases of the nervous system, and influenza, and that ended indigestion, cleared the skin, brightened the eyes, and conferred abounding health on all who imbibed it. It was available at modest expense from every drugstore in Essenheim.

Then, in the voice of one who could hardly believe himself to be so immensely privileged, the announcer

121

said that a distinguished visitor to Essenheim was here in the studio with him. He greeted Kate in English. She replied in moderately fluent Essenheimisch. This was a great success. The announcer became almost incoherent with enthusiasm. He congratulated Kate three times over on her excellent accent, repeated his appreciation of the honor conferred on him by her presence, and asked her what she thought of Essenheim. Kate replied that she liked it. This verdict was received with rapture, and the interview proceeded from height to height. Kate herself began to feel that her appearance on Radio Essenheim was a milestone in its history.

After seven minutes, with an eye on the studio clock, the announcer thanked Kate effusively and announced that there would be a live broadcast of Thursday's reception. He finished talking precisely on the hour, and activated a signal that sounded uncannily like a door chime.

"And now, Essenheimers," he went on, "your world news bulletin."

Kate listened, wondering which items of world news would most interest the people of Essenheim. It seemed in fact that their world was a small one. There wasn't anything about international affairs. The bulletin began with an item about a peasant who'd fallen into a stream on his way home from the wine cellar and had ruined his Sunday suit. It continued with news of a crime wave that had hit Essenheim—the Town Magistrate had sent two people to prison for five days each, on separate charges of creating public disturbances. They were Aleksi Wandervogel, poet, and Countess Sonia Zackendorf, university teacher. The bulletin continued with two or three further local items before the announcer sounded his door chime again and began to extol the virtues of Willi Bamberger's used car lot, just behind the town hall.

The station director came into the studio, finger on lips, and led Kate away. The announcer gave her a thumbs-up sign as she left.

"He seems very enthusiastic," Kate said to the station director.

"Moritz? I should hope he does. That's what we pay him for."

"Did you hear," Kate asked Rudi on the way back to the castle, "about the arrests?"

"What arrests?"

"Aleksi and Sonia. Sent to prison for five days for causing public disturbances."

Rudi swore in Essenheimisch. "They'll still be there on the day of the reception," he said. "They'll yell the place down. You can hear shouting from those cells all over the castle."

"You mean they're in the castle dungeons?" asked Kate.

"Yes. The dungeons serve as lockup for the whole Principality."

"Are there many people shut up there now?"

"Oh, no. Except at festivals and the wine harvest, when we get a few drunks, the cells are mostly empty."

When he'd parked the car, Rudi took Kate in through

the side door by which she'd first entered the castle—
long ago, as it now seemed—and led her through the
echoing old kitchens and down a flight of spiral stone
steps. At the bottom, a stout wooden door blocked the
way.

"The wine cellars are beyond this," Rudi said by way
of explanation. "There's enough wine and brandy down
here to keep the entire population drunk for a decade.
Maxi!" he yelled. "Maxi!"

Shouts from the prisoners could now be heard, and
then a small, thin, middle-aged man opened the heavy
wooden door. "Highness?" he said, bowing.

"Meet Maxi," Rudi said to Kate. "He is both our
jailer and the keeper of the wine cellars." To Maxi
himself he said, "So you have some prisoners, eh?"

"Yes, Highness. Herr Wandervogel was reciting his
stuff in the marketplace. Annoying the passersby, the
policeman said. That probably means he was annoying
the policeman. Those two don't get on together at all.
Somehow poetry and policing don't mix."

"And Countess Zackendorf?"

"She was parading the High Street with a sign saying
'Down with the fascist Prince!'"

"Why should she be arrested for that? It's supposed
to be a free country."

"Yes, Highness, but she'd taken the sign from Frau
Schmidt's front garden and painted her slogan on the
back of it. It was a nice new sign saying 'Ritz-Albany
Hotel.' Countess Zackendorf said she'd only borrowed
it, but the Magistrate sent her down just the same."

Maxi led the way along a stone-flagged passage to

124

a row of cells. Kate shivered in the dungeon chill. The faces of the prisoners could be seen at the tiny openings in the doors of the first two cells.

As soon as he saw them, Aleksi began to declaim in dramatic tones some lines that Kate translated from the Essenheimisch as "Prisons are constructed without any stone in the walls, and cages without iron bars." She tried to puzzle it out. Then it dawned on her.

" 'Stone walls do not a prison make,' " she said, " 'Nor iron bars a cage.' "

"That's right!" Aleksi said delightly. "Richard Lovelace, the Cavalier poet. One of the influences on my work."

"Cavaliers!" cried Sonia in disgust. "Aristocrats! I spit on them!"

"We must get these two out of here," said Rudi. "I know what I'll do. I'll just slip upstairs to Uncle and get him to write out a royal pardon. I won't be a minute."

"In the meantime, please step into my humble abode, gracious young lady," Maxi said to Kate. "Do me the honor of meeting my wife and daughter."

Just off the passage was a cheerful room with a big stone fireplace, in which burned a much-needed coal fire. In front of the fire sat a buxom girl of about twenty with black hair, red cheeks, and bold brown eyes. From a room beyond, presumably the kitchen, emerged a massively built woman of similar coloring, obviously the girl's mother. She was not so much fat as immensely muscular; she dominated Maxi completely and made her buxom daughter look slim. She curtseyed with heavyweight agility. "My wife, Bertha," Maxi said. "My daughter, Bettina."

The girl was looking at Kate with interest and some slight hostility. "So you're Rudi's new girl friend," she said.

"*Prince* Rudi to you, my girl!" her mother told her. "Don't be familiar with your betters!"

Bettina tossed her head defiantly.

"She gets ideas above her station," Bertha told Kate. "Not that our family's to be sniffed at, mind you, with Maxi in his position and me being head cleaning woman for the whole castle. Now, gracious young lady, I'm sure you'd like a nice cup of coffee. I've just made some."

Kate was sipping coffee and listening to an account of the responsibilities of a head cleaning woman when Rudi returned with a piece of paper in his hand—presumably the pardon from the Prince Laureate. Kate wondered whether there was a swift exchange of glances between him and Bettina, or whether she was drawing wrong conclusions. And then she realized that she'd heard Bettina's voice before. It was that of the woman who'd been sitting on the terrace in the moonlight with Rudi, on Kate's first night in Essenheim.

Maxi accepted the piece of paper and went along to the cells, jingling his keys. But it seemed that the prisoners didn't want to leave. They were quite comfortable, they declared. Sonia accused Rudi of trying to evict them without notice, in a manner typical of a fascist state. When Kate and Rudi left the dungeons, the cell doors were open but Aleksi and Sonia were still inside, respectively declaiming and complaining, while Maxi appealed to them in vain to come out.

"They'll leave before long," Rudi assured Kate as they climbed the stone steps. "They're making plenty of fuss, but now they've been pardoned there won't be any food for them. They'll go home when they're hungry."

17

─────── ❧❦ ───────

The afternoon before the reception, it occurred to Kate that she still hadn't been up the tower. Rudi had disappeared on some of the unexplained business that took him away from the castle from time to time. Kate proposed the ascent to Anni, but she was not enthusiastic.

"Those steps go on *forever*," she said. "I went up once. I was *dizzy* and I was *exhausted*, and there's nothing when you get there except a view of Essenheim. And you want to know what views of Essenheim do for me? Nothing, that's what they do for me, nothing. I'd rather have a view of a London shopping street." It was clear that she would prefer to play her records while Kate did the climbing.

"Send for Maxi," she suggested.

Maxi was summoned, and arrived jingling a bunch of keys. He led Kate through the Great Hall and along two or three corridors until they came to a massive wooden door, bolted and barred. Maxi raised two bars, drew two massive bolts, chose and inserted a key, and opened the door.

"Shall I come with you, gracious young lady?" he asked. "It's gloomy in there. There's no light in the tower except what comes in through those tiny windows. Ladies usually need a man with them, so as not to be frightened."

"*I* don't need a man with me, thank you very much," said Kate. "I'm not easily frightened."

"Very well, gracious young lady. There are one hundred ninety-seven steps from here to the top. If you count them on the way down, you'll know you're back at the right floor. And here, if you're on your own, you're going to need a key."

He detached one from his bunch. "It's a spare," he said, "but don't forget to give it back to me. It opens this door, and the one at the top of the tower onto the roof, and the door into the basement from the old kitchens. Anyone who has this key can get into the dungeons and wine cellars. So take care of it, gracious young lady, please. And be careful on those steps!"

The door swung behind Kate with a solid-sounding *clunk*. In spite of what she'd said about not being afraid, she felt a moment's unease.

She was on a small stone landing, from which a flight of spiral steps led upward and another led down into the depths. A little light filtered in through a slit window. Maxi hadn't exaggerated when he'd said it was gloomy.

She set off on the upward climb. The staircase was fairly wide at first; there were window slits at regular intervals, and periodically she came to a landing like

129

the one she'd started from, with a locked door to some other level. Then the landings ceased and the spiral became so tight that she had to place her feet sideways and began to suffer from vertigo. Obviously she was now in the high, narrow part of the tower.

It took a long time to climb the 197 steps, and Kate was both tired and dizzy by the time she reached the top. The stairway ended at a locked door. Straining her eyes in the half-light, Kate found the keyhole, inserted the key that Maxi had given her, opened the door, and stepped out into blinding sunlight. There was just room enough to stand between the parapets.

Kate blinked. When her eyes became used to the light, she could see that the view was indeed spectacular. Directly beneath her was the sheer east wall of the castle, plunging to the river gorge far below. Across the gorge, the Low Town clung crazily to such precarious ledges as would accommodate streets and buildings. From the western parapet she saw the newer quarters of the town, the High Street, the market square, the bridge across the chasm, the airstrip, the antenna of the radio station. Beyond the town on all sides were the hills and valleys of Essenheim, and beyond those the high mountains that cut the Principality off from the world.

Alone on this high tower, Kate had a sudden sharp sense of isolation. She didn't want to stay up here long. She went inside again, locked the door behind her, and in the dim light from the slit windows made her way cautiously down the spiral staircase. Partway down she realized that she'd forgotten to start counting the

197 steps, but she didn't feel like going back to the top and beginning again. She thought she knew roughly where she'd got to.

But she was deceived by the difference between the toilsome ascent and the easier descent. She was just beginning to think she must be getting near her point of entry to the tower when she realized that light was reaching the staircase from an open door. She had come too far and was only a few steps from the bottom. The door, through which she could see a stone-flagged passage, presumably led into the basement where the dungeons and wine cellars were.

Kate wondered for a moment whether to go back up the steps and look for the door at which she'd come in. But she didn't know how far up it was, and felt a strong disinclination to return to the gloom of the staircase. Surely if she went out into the basement she would soon find Maxi's quarters? She could give him back his key and return to civilization through the old kitchens.

She walked out of the tower and along the passage. On either side of it were rows of empty cells. Silence lay thick as dust and was hardly disturbed by Kate's feet in their soft shoes.

Eventually the passageway branched. Each branch was similarly lit by low-powered light bulbs; there was nothing to indicate which would be more likely to take her to a way out. At random she took the left-hand branch, and soon found that she was in among the wine cellars. Room after room, though empty of people, was full of barrels: hundreds of barrels, barrels

131

beyond counting. Prince Ferdinand Franz Josef III of Essenheim might be a poor man, but he seemed to have a wealth of wine and brandy. Enough to keep the entire population drunk for a decade, Rudi had said. She could believe it.

Kate went back to the point at which the passage had branched and took the other direction. Here there were more empty cells. She shivered, feeling the dank stone chill of the place and regretting her decision to leave the staircase. The passage ran into another one, which in turn led into a third. But finally she realized thankfully that she'd come to a part of the basement she had been in before. She was passing the row of cells where Aleksi and Sonia had been locked up.

She continued, and came to the door of Maxi's apartment. It was closed. She tapped on it confidently. Nobody came. She knocked more loudly. Still nobody came. Well, she could find her way out from here. But she banged on the door once more, just for luck. And this time somebody came and opened it.

Rudi.

His expression was startled. He seemed on the point of closing the door in her face. Then, holding it just a little ajar, he said, "Kate! What *are* you doing down here?"

Kate began to explain, but hadn't even finished a sentence when a rough female voice came from inside the room. "Oh, let them in, whoever it is!" the voice called.

Rudi spoke a cross word in Essenheimisch and reluc-

132

tantly opened the door wide. As before, there was a blazing fire in the room. In her seat at the chimney corner was Maxi's daughter Bettina. She looked slightly disheveled. And Kate knew as well as if she'd seen it that Rudi and Bettina had been embracing.

Bettina looked sour but not embarrassed. "Oh, it's you, gracious young lady," she said. On her lips the phrase sounded like an insult. "You've found your boy friend, haven't you? And now you're finding that he's mine as well!"

Rudi said to Kate, uneasily, "Take no notice of Tina, she's a joker."

Bettina said, "Oh, yes, sure, it's all a joke. You can hear me laughing, can't you? Kiss and make up, that's Rudi, and he always gets away with it."

Kate said coldly, "I got lost, Rudi. I was in the tower and I came down too far."

"I'll show you the way back upstairs," Rudi said.

"It's all right. I can find it for myself."

"Let me come with you, all the same."

Out in the passageway, Rudi said, "There's a simple explanation."

"I expect there is," said Kate. "But don't bother to give it."

"Oh, Kate!" He tried to take her hand, but she pulled it away.

"I know just where I am, Rudi," she said. "In more ways than one. I shall stay over Thursday so as not to embarrass your uncle. And then I'm going."

"I'm sorry . . ." Rudi began.

133

"That's all right," said Kate with all the dignity she could muster. "You don't have to apologize. It's your life. But I'm not playing any more part in it. *Please* don't come with me now."

And she walked away from him.

18

There was heavy rain in Essenheim on the morning of the reception, but everyone assured Kate that it wouldn't last; and it didn't. In midmorning the thick cover of clouds drew slowly back across the sky like a great curtain, revealing a brilliant expanse of blue. Streets and roofs shone in the sunlight; the trees along the avenue that led from castle gate to market square glistened green in the newly freshened air.

Kate and Rudi hardly spoke to each other that morning. Once or twice he looked at her with mute appeal; other times he seemed tense and preoccupied. The old Prince, however, was in good spirits. After lunch he took Kate to the window of his private room, which had a balcony looking out over the main forecourt and the avenue into town. Flags were flying and streamers hung across the street saying LONG LIVE OUR PRINCE and HAPPY ANNIVERSARY and 30 GLORIOUS YEARS. People were already gathering in the open space before the castle, and the Principality's little squad of police were all on duty, controlling them. As Kate watched, a shout of "Prince! Prince! Prince!" was set up.

"I must go out and wave," the Prince Laureate said.

Cheers rose from the crowd as he went out onto the balcony. He turned and beckoned to Kate to join him. Doubtfully she went out, to be greeted with more cheering. Everyone seemed to know who she was.

There were tears in the old man's eyes when, after repeated waves from him and shouts of acclaim from below, he finally limped inside. "They still love their old Prince," he said. "I'm not a great man, you know. I was born to this job; I didn't get it on merit. But I've done my best. They'll miss me when I'm gone."

Kate found herself kissing his cheek. "There, there," she said. "You won't be gone for years and years yet."

"You can't deceive me, my dear," the Prince said. "I'm not in good shape." He shot a sideways glance at her. "I believe Rudi told you of our plans."

"Yes," said Kate.

"He shouldn't have, really. But I'm sure I can trust you."

"I haven't told anyone," said Kate.

"Of course you haven't. You are the soul of discretion."

He smiled affectionately. "And now, I must rest for an hour or so, if I am to carry out my duties this afternoon. I advise you to do the same, Kate. You will find the occasion rather demanding."

Kate hadn't taken afternoon rests since she was in kindergarten, but when she got to her room the bed

136

seemed suddenly tempting, and she decided she'd lie
on it for ten minutes, though she wouldn't go to sleep.
The next thing she knew was being shaken by Anni.

"Wake up, wake up, Kate. They're starting to arrive!"

Kate sat up, blinking. "And we haven't changed!"
she said. Anni was still in jeans.

"We won't be needed in the first hour," Anni told
her. "I've been to these affairs before. Rudi as heir
to the throne and Dr. Stockhausen as Prime Minister
welcome the guests; that's the way it's done here. Then
they all tuck into the food and wine. Uncle Ferdy appears later on the dais and makes his little speech.
All it amounts to is 'Hello, folks,' but they all applaud
like it was Shakespeare. After that you and I come
on as the supporting cast, to brighten up the show.
Uncle introduces us, as if they didn't all know who
we are already. And then we and Uncle circulate, saying polite nothings to everyone in sight. All you have
to remember is not to swear and not to say anything
that matters."

"I can't swear in Essenheimisch anyway," said Kate.

"Remind me tomorrow and I'll teach you. And now
come with me and we'll watch them arriving. I know
a perfect spy spot."

Anni led the way into her own room, a couple of
doors away from Kate's. She opened a tall cupboard
and casually slid aside a panel in the back of it.

"What on earth . . . ?" began Kate.

"Don't look so startled," Anni said, taking a flashlight
from a shelf. "It's only a secret passage. Great-great-

137

grandpa had lots of them built into the castle, and I know more than anybody else. They come in handy sometimes."

Kate squeezed her way along the narrow passage behind Anni. They went round a corner and continued for some distance before Anni signaled Kate to a halt. They were at a superb vantage point. On one side of the passage a slit window in the castle's outer wall gave an excellent view of the main forecourt; at the other side the interior of the Great Hall could be seen through a narrow opening in a dusky recess, invisible to anyone on the floor of the hall. Guests could be seen arriving in the forecourt, and observed again a few minutes later as they entered the hall.

Kate watched with fascination, and Anni provided a running commentary. Some thirty royal cousins and other aristocracy arrived in carriages drawn by large, plodding horses; "They usually pull the winery drays," Anni explained. The gentlemen wore knee breeches and embroidered velvet coats; the ladies were in full, brocaded silk gowns, some with bustles. The finery had a slightly dusty look, suggesting to Kate a period play put on by an amateur dramatic society with limited funds.

The professional guests were sharply distinguished from the aristocracy: The men wore mostly black coats and striped trousers, and the women long evening dress. Some arrived in chauffeur-driven cars, some drove their own, and the handful of decrepit town taxis made several appearances. On one of these trips a soberly suited George was disgorged. A minority of the humbler guests arrived on mopeds, by bicycle, and on foot.

"The cream of Essenheim society is all here now," Anni remarked. She didn't seem particularly impressed.

From the opening in the dim recess, Kate watched the guests being received. As they were announced, they were greeted by Rudi at one side of the door and by Dr. Stockhausen at the other. Kate caught her breath on first beholding Rudi, who looked more splendid than ever. His dress upstaged everyone else's. It was a little later in period than the rest: He wore a crimson cutaway coat and tight-fitting white trousers that fastened at the ankle. Kate, who knew her Jane Austen, thought he looked like a younger and sprightlier Mr. Darcy. As he bent over the hands of curtseying ladies, she was sure they were all in love with him.

Gradually the forecourt emptied and the hall filled. The guests headed eagerly for the food, which did indeed look very good. Most of the castle staff had been pressed into service as waiters or waitresses, and circulated gracefully or gracelessly according to their abilities. There was an air of faded splendor about the scene—the twilight of the once-great Hohlbergs.

Kate was musing on this when Anni dug her in the ribs and said, "Come on. Our turn now." They stumbled back along the secret passage.

An anxious Chamberlain (the dark-suited person who'd greeted Kate on her first arrival at the castle) was waiting to hurry Kate and Anni and was glancing

White Rabbit-like at his watch; and the little round-eyed maid, Lilli, hovered between Kate's room and Anni's, trying to help them dress. It didn't take them long to put on the black and the white silk nightgowns. Kate had a moment's dreadful doubt about the suitability of these, but Lilli seemed to admire them.

In his private sitting room the old Prince was waiting for them. His ceremonial Army uniform didn't flatter his sagging form; he looked a little pathetic, and his spirits had drooped.

"Well, it's the last time," he said with a kind of mournful satisfaction. "Rudi says when he's Prince Laureate he'll stop the dressing up."

"I'll bet he won't," said Anni. "Costume suits him too well."

The Prince grunted. Then, looking from Anni to Kate and back, he grew more cheerful. "You look beautiful, my dears," he told them. "Beautiful. You could marry Emperors and do them credit, both of you, if only there were a few Emperors left."

He offered his right arm to Anni and his left to Kate. Preceded by the Chamberlain, they moved from the private apartments along a gallery and down the main staircase, which Kate had not previously used. She had a momentary wild impulse to detach herself from the Prince Laureate and slide down the bannister; she wouldn't actually have done it, but she thought Anni might. For the moment, however, Anni was demure and dignified. A few guests had wandered out of the Great Hall and respectfully watched their descent. At the foot of the staircase Rudi and Friedrich joined

140

them. Gentlemen bowed and ladies curtseyed as they passed.

The Chamberlain went ahead through the double doors into the Great Hall. The band struck up the national anthem, "Heaven Help Essenheim." This was set to a mournful tune that contrived to suggest that heaven would have its work cut out for it. The Chamberlain went to the microphone.

"It's working," whispered Rudi. "Hurrah!"

"His Illustrious Highness, Prince Ferdinand Franz Josef the Third," the Chamberlain announced. He intoned the Prince's titles: Prince Laureate of Essenheim, Duke of Teufelwald, Count of the Two Rivers, Baron Schatztal, and two or three others there hadn't been room for on the invitations. The Prince himself shambled forward, to spontaneous applause. Dr. Stockhausen approached him, bent a knee, and read a loyal address in his dry accountant's tones. The Prince went up to the microphone amid cheers. Somebody adjusted it for him.

"My dear people," he began. There was renewed cheering. "It is a great joy to come before you once more, after thirty years spent in your service as Prince Laureate, to say how deeply I am touched and honored by your loyalty."

The Prince reminisced for a few minutes about some of the principal events of his reign. Rudi, standing beside Kate at the back of the dais, looked anxious and impatient, and at one point muttered so that only Kate could hear, "I wish he'd get on with it!" She wondered for a moment whether it was possible that the old

141

Prince, moved by the applause, would change his mind and not abdicate after all. But finally he half turned and motioned Rudi forward to join him.

"You will all know," he said, "that my nephew Prince Rudolf has lately returned to the Principality. It was my intention today to reaffirm his position as Crown Prince, heir to the throne of Essenheim."

There was a little scattered applause, which the Prince halted with a gesture.

"I have, however," he said, "come to a different decision."

Kate, watching Dr. Stockhausen's face, saw a startled expression come to it.

"I am an old man," the Prince Laureate went on, "a tired man. The time has come to say that I have done enough. I now announce to you my abdication with effect from this moment, and the accession of Prince Rudolf to the throne." He turned and said in a firm voice, "Rudolf, step forward."

Rudi knelt before him. The old Prince raised him to his feet. "Rudolf Wilhelm Hohlberg," he said, "I renounce my throne to you, and proclaim you from this moment Prince Laureate of Essenheim." In his turn he knelt down. "And I declare myself your loyal subject."

There was a stunned silence all through the Great Hall. The ex-Prince Laureate struggled painfully to his feet. Then suddenly Dr. Stockhausen was at the microphone.

"I cannot allow it!" he declared in sharp, ringing tones. "The constitution of Essenheim does not provide

for abdication. The law must be changed before anything like this can happen!"

Rudi grabbed the microphone from him. Dr. Stockhausen tried to get it back, and Rudi pushed him away.

"The monarch is absolute!" Rudi proclaimed. "He
can do as he wishes. He *has* done as he wished. I speak
to you as your Prince Laureate. I expect and demand
your loyalty!"

There was an outbreak of loud excited talk all over
the hall. No one seemed to know what to make of
the events. Dr. Stockhausen returned to the attack.

"You are not Prince Laureate!" he told Rudi. "Not
yet!"

Then the bulky form of Colonel Schweiner stepped
from the floor to the dais. There was a pistol in his
hand. He strode up to Dr. Stockhausen, placed the
pistol at his head, and fired. The explosion, so close
to the microphone, was deafening. It looked for a moment as though Schweiner had shot the Prime Minister.
But Stockhausen didn't fall to the ground. He stepped
back a pace, unsteady with shock, and stared unbelievingly into Schweiner's face.

"That," said Schweiner, "was a blank. Another time,
it would not be a blank. Heinrich von Stockhausen,
you are under arrest!"

Soldiers were swarming onto the dais. Two of them
seized Stockhausen by the arms. He seemed too startled to resist.

"Colonel Schweiner!" Rudi's voice was loud and indignant. "What are you doing? I don't require this kind
of help from you! It is disgraceful!"

"You too are under arrest, Rudolf Hohlberg!" said Schweiner; and then, into the microphone: "The Army has taken over!"

There were cries of outrage among the royal guests, and a surge toward the dais, but the movement suddenly lost impetus when it was seen that Schweiner's men were everywhere. The entire Essenheim Army of sixty appeared to be in the hall, and every man had a gun. On the galleries surrounding the Great Hall were soldiers with machine guns. One of them, by design or accident, fired a burst into the ceiling.

"Stay where you are!" Schweiner ordered the guests. "Anyone who moves will be shot."

More and more soldiers had mounted the dais. Two of Schweiner's men seized Rudi. He struggled, and one of them hit him on the head with the butt of his gun. Rudi slumped to the ground. Two more men dragged a kicking, screaming Anni from the dais. The old Prince, the Prime Minister, and Friedrich had already been hustled away. And now rough arms went round Kate from behind.

"This way, gracious young lady!" said a soldier's voice in her ear. "You too are under arrest. You are to be taken to your room until further orders from the Colonel!"

A hand was slapped across Kate's mouth. As she was marched from the dais and away through the double doors, she heard shouting from the hall, followed by three or four more single shots and then Schweiner's voice again at the microphone.

"It is no good resisting!" he was telling the assembled

guests. "The party is over. Those of you who wish to leave the room alive will swear loyalty to me and then go quietly to your homes. I, Hermann Schweiner, am ruler of Essenheim!"

19

For five or ten minutes after the door of Kate's room had closed behind her, the shouting continued. She heard several more shots, one alarming scream cut off in the middle, and the tramping of a good many feet. And then there was silence, a total silence that soon began to seem uncanny. Kate sat on her bed, shocked and bewildered and unable quite to believe what had happened, though her lips and cheeks still hurt from the pressure of the soldier's hand.

One of the men who'd brought her there had vanished. The other—the raw recruit who had been given such a hard time on the parade ground—stood just inside Kate's door, watching her. Her legs felt like water, but after a few minutes, with enormous effort, she got up and made as if to leave the room. The soldier stopped her.

"I'm sorry, gracious young lady," he said, "but you aren't allowed to go. It isn't me that says so, it's orders. Colonel's orders."

"What is *happening*?" she asked him shakily.

"The Colonel has taken power. It was his patriotic duty. He told us so."

Kate went back to her bed. She sat for a few minutes, still suffering from shock, then felt that she had to do something, whether useful or not. She went into the tiny bathroom, thankful to have this amount of privacy, and changed into everyday clothes. Then she turned the radio on. A rough male voice could be heard in altercation with the announcer, Moritz. Kate turned up the volume. The male voice, triumphant, said, "Everybody stay at home. Wait for instructions. The Army is in control." Some elderly pop music—Radio Essenheim's standard fare—followed this. Then the voice of Moritz came through in its usual tones of bright excitement and cheerful salesmanship.

"Essenheimers," Moritz said, "it's a great day for the Principality. The former Principality, I should say. Freedom has come to Essenheim. The dead hand of the Hohlberg monarchy has been removed from the people's throats. Colonel Schweiner has taken control. The future of the nation is no longer at risk. Peace and prosperity lie ahead of us. To ease the transition, there will be a curfew in Essenheim town until dawn tomorrow. Anyone who goes out will be shot."

Moritz presented this last piece of information as if it were an amazing bargain offer, not to be missed. Then he added that Colonel Schweiner would address the nation at nine that evening. Kate switched the radio off.

The young soldier had been listening with her. Kate

147

asked him, "What about the old Prince? And Prince Rudi and Princess Anni and Prince Friedrich? And Dr. Stockhausen? What's happened to them?"

"I don't know, gracious young lady. I don't know any more than you do. I just do as I'm told."

Kate reviewed her own position. Surely she herself could not be detained for long . . . or could she? What about George? Had he been arrested too? Even if he was at large, could he get news of the coup out of Essenheim?

Come on, Kate! she told herself. Don't just sit here. Think what you can *do*! The trouble was that she couldn't think of *anything* to do except await developments.

A little later another soldier appeared with food for her. It was a plate piled high with hors d'oeuvres, crackers, peanuts, canapés, cocktail sausages, and other leftovers from the reception. Kate had little appetite, but when you didn't know what was going to happen next it seemed like a good idea to eat while you could. She finished every scrap.

Shortly before nine Kate switched the radio on again. Moritz was delivering a commercial. It all sounded just as usual. But then came the door chime, followed by the ponderous opening notes of "Heaven Help Essenheim." Moritz announced, "The President of the Revolutionary Council, Savior of the Nation, and Leader of the People of Essenheim, His Excellency, Colonel Hermann Schweiner."

A pause. And then the pompous, overbearing tones

148

that brought to Kate a sudden, repellent recollection of the man's physical presence.

"Essenheimers, the revolution is complete! I, Hermann Schweiner, have led it to success! I, Hermann Schweiner, promise you that the old, dishonored regime of the Hohlbergs is at an end! I, Hermann Schweiner, will revive the nation as I have revived the Army! Essenheim, though small, will be great!"

The odious voice went on and on. The address was all about the power and glory of Schweiner. At the end of the broadcast, almost as an afterthought, came the information that the pretender to the throne, Prince Rudi, would be put on trial for crimes against the state. The ex-Prince Laureate would be spared because of his age, and flown out to Serenia. Nothing was said of Anni, Friedrich, or Dr. Stockhausen. Or of Kate herself.

"That," said Moritz in the bright tones of one introducing a unique new product, "was the leader of our nation, Colonel Hermann Schweiner." He added with patriotic fervor, "Heaven help Essenheim!"

The opening bars of the anthem were repeated. Kate switched the radio off. In another minute she'd have been throwing things at it. Her resentment against Rudi had evaporated and she was white-faced with fury. "Tried for crimes against the state!" she echoed. "Oh, Rudi!"

She turned on the young soldier who was guarding her. "What's your name?" she demanded.

"Willi, gracious young lady. Private Willi Braun."

149

"Let me out of here, Willi Braun! At once! Let me out, I tell you!" She put all the passion and authority she could into her voice. The young soldier trembled, but he didn't give way. A minute later Kate found herself sobbing violently.

After half an hour she had sobbed herself into a frustrated silence. Then suddenly the door burst open and Schweiner himself strode in. The young soldier sprang to attention.

"Out!" ordered Schweiner. "On the double!" Willi went. Schweiner turned to Kate.

"Get up, get up!" he told her.

Kate got up from her bed. Schweiner misinterpreted her look of loathing. "Don't be afraid," he said. "I'm not going to hurt you."

"I'm not afraid," said Kate. "Where are the people you arrested?"

"The old Prince is in the cells until we fly him out. Rudi, Friedrich, and Stockhausen are also in the cells, awaiting trial. Princess Anni, like you, is confined to her room until I decide what to do with her. But never mind them. I didn't come here to talk about them. They are yesterday's people."

"And *you* are today's? Heaven help Essenheim!"

Schweiner wagged a finger at her. "Now, now, gracious young lady. Calm yourself and be respectful. You are talking to the ruler of the country. Everything is under my control. A few stupid people resisted and had to be put in the dungeons, but it's all quiet now. The change is irreversible. Firm rule and unquestionable authority are what the people need, and I, Schweiner, will give it to them." Then a smirk came to his face.

"As for *you*, gracious young lady, you may care to know that I have a soft spot for you. It could even be said that I, Hermann Schweiner, *like* you."

Kate felt the urge to throw his liking straight back in his face, but restrained herself and said, "Then let my friends go."

"I am not discussing that," said Schweiner. "Let us discuss *you*, instead. It is more than possible that you yourself have a future in this country."

"What do you mean?" Kate asked, startled.

"I am a widower, gracious young lady. A widower, Kate. And I am considering remarriage."

"That has nothing to do with me!"

"Ah, but it could have," said Schweiner. He looked at her with a benevolent expression that almost turned her stomach. "I am no longer, perhaps, in my first youth. Indeed, I confess that the age of fifty now lies behind me. But I am still a fine figure of a man, in the prime of life!"

"Are you proposing to me?" Kate asked, aghast.

"Not quite. Not yet. Do not jump to conclusions. Do not, as we say in Essenheim, count your eggs while they are still in the chicken. But it is a possibility."

"Oh, no, it's not!" said Kate.

Schweiner didn't understand that she was expressing horror at the idea. He thought she couldn't believe her luck. His smile became still more hideous.

"In the Essenheim of Hermann Schweiner," he said, "all things are possible."

Kate passed a restless night and awoke with a headache. She found that the guard had been changed; Willi had gone, and in his place was a dark, scowling young man who didn't answer her greeting. Her breakfast, however, was fresh coffee and rolls, and later she was brought a decent lunch of cold meat.

Her link with the outside world, such as it was, was the little radio on her dressing table. Kate didn't know how long its batteries would last, and used it cautiously. The programs from Radio Essenheim seemed once again deceptively normal. But soon after noon Moritz interrupted himself with a special announcement. In order to pay for Essenheim's coming prosperity, it said, all taxes would be raised by half.

In the early evening the new guard went off duty and Willi returned. He smiled sheepishly at Kate, but when she asked him what had been happening in the town, he couldn't tell her anything; nor did he have any information on the royal prisoners.

Kate had no appetite for her supper, which was a thick Essenheimisch stew. And after supper Schweiner appeared once more and banished the trembling Willi to the far side of the door.

Schweiner seemed to have puffed himself up to even greater and more froglike proportions. He wore a familiar-looking uniform, covered with medals and insignia of rank. Seeing Kate's eyes on this, he remarked, "Yes, it's the old Prince's."

"But . . . the Prince was wearing it at the reception."

"Yes. He's in his underpants now. There's nothing like taking away a man's dignity if you want to keep him quiet."

"That's horrible! And anyway, I thought he was being flown out to Serenia."

"Perhaps, young lady, perhaps. I'm having second thoughts about that. There have been new developments since last night. One of them was unfortunate." He frowned. "Somebody got into the dungeons and let Dr. Stockhausen and Prince Friedrich out."

"I'm glad!" said Kate.

"They'll be found, gracious young lady. It's only a matter of time. However, let's not dwell on that minor annoyance. I have far more important news for you, Kate. Prepare to congratulate me. I am to become the father of a Princess!"

"You're *what?*" said Kate, staring.

"I am to be the father of a Princess. And father-in-law of a Prince."

"But . . . how?"

"By marriage, dear Kate. That is the other development since last night. A happy one. Prince Rudi is to marry my daughter Elsa!"

"You're joking," Kate said faintly.

"I am not joking. Elsa went to see him in his cell this morning. He proposed to her and she accepted him. Now he has been released. He is to remain Prince Laureate, and Elsa will be the Princess Laureate. Their engagement will be announced on the radio tomorrow and in the *Essenheim Free Press* on Tuesday."

153

"You mean," Kate said incredulously, "that Rudi has bought his freedom and his title back by agreeing to marry Elsa?"

"I don't like your way of putting it," said Schweiner, frowning. "He will get a good and suitable wife. Elsa is a fine girl, fit to bear future Princes."

"And *you* will rule the roost!"

"I shall govern Essenheim," Schweiner agreed. "Essenheim needs me."

Kate pulled herself together as best she could. "What about the old Prince and Anni?" she asked. "Aren't they included in the deal?"

"There is no 'deal,'" said Schweiner. "I would not have entered into a deal with Rudi over his relatives even if he had asked me. That would have been sordid. Besides, since Rudi has been freed, and Stockhausen and Friedrich have escaped, I need someone to put on trial. It may have to be the old Prince."

"You *have* to put someone on trial?"

"Of course. It is the mark of a new regime. We must expose the villainy of the old one. So you see, Kate, when you ask that Prince Ferdinand be freed, you are asking a great deal. What do you offer in return?"

"Nothing," said Kate.

"Nothing? In this world one doesn't get anything for nothing." Schweiner looked knowingly at Kate. "There is a way in which you can save the old Prince and Princess Anni. And I think you know what it is!"

"Not . . . ?"

"Yes. By marrying me. I now formally propose to

you. I shall return tomorrow evening, by which time I shall expect your decision. And be warned, gracious young lady. Hermann Schweiner does not gladly take 'No' for an answer."

20

Five minutes after Schweiner had left Kate's room, there was a tap at the door. Willi stood aside to admit Rudi, now wearing an officer's uniform.

"Oh. It's you," said Kate.

"Don't look so disapproving, dear Kate," said Rudi. He smiled his most disarming smile. "I've come to see what I can do for you."

"And I suppose your prospective father-in-law sent you?" Kate said. "Well, I'll tell you what you can do. You can get me out of here, and your uncle and Anni as well, and you can put us all on a plane for Serenia. Now. Immediately."

"It's not as simple as that. You must try to realize that Schweiner's in charge, I'm not. The Army obeys him, not me."

"Then why are you playing his game?"

"The Schweiner coup has happened, Kate. It's no good wishing it hadn't. My aim now is to have a restraining influence. There's no telling what he might get up to on his own."

"So you've done it all for the best, I suppose?"

"Well, yes, actually," said Rudi. He put on his most appealing look. Kate yearned to believe him, and almost achieved it. But she hardened her heart.

"And you have your reward," she said. "The title of Prince Laureate, and a charming bride. I wish you joy of Elsa Schweiner."

Rudi winced. "I hope it won't come to that," he said. "I shan't let the wedding day be fixed for very soon, I can assure you. In the meantime I have other cards to play. I don't really see myself as son-in-law to Schweiner. And although I know his intentions, I don't see you as Schweiner's wife."

"Thank goodness for that."

"But I think that for the present you should go along with him. Let him believe that if he persists he'll succeed in the end. I know Schweiner. If you reject him, he'll turn nasty, perhaps very nasty. That's my sincere advice, Kate."

"I don't want your advice, Rudi. I just want to be let out of here."

"I will speak to Schweiner," Rudi said. And without another word he turned and let himself out of the room. Willi placed his back to the door in case Kate showed signs of following. Kate didn't know whether, if Rudi had stayed another few seconds, she'd have hit him or thrown herself weeping into his arms. As it was, she went to sit once more on the bed, and thought hard for a long time.

One of the subjects of her thought was Willi. At some stage he had brought a little stool from the bathroom, and he now sat on it just beside the doorway, looking blankly at nothing in particular. She got up and went over to him. As their eyes met, he gave her an uncertain smile.

"What do *you* think of all this, Willi?" she asked him. "All these goings-on in the castle?"

"I don't think about them, gracious young lady. I'm not paid to think. That's what the Colonel tells us all every day."

"You let him do the thinking for you?"

"Yes, gracious young lady. Well, he's in command, isn't he? Thinking's his job. We just do as he tells us."

"And you—you and the other soldiers—you're not likely to rebel against him?"

Willi looked shocked. "Oh, *no*, gracious young lady. Certainly not!" He added thoughtfully, "Though I must say, some of them are a bit disappointed."

"Oh!" said Kate with interest. "What about?"

"Well, they'd got it into their heads that when the Army took power they'd be allowed into the castle cellars to drink all they wished. There's supposed to be thousands of liters of good Essenheim wine and brandy down there."

Kate recalled the barrels she'd seen, and thought millions of liters might be more like it. "And what actually happened?" she asked.

"The Colonel said they'd misunderstood him. He never intended to let them loose in the cellars. And I must say, considering what some of them are like when they drink, I'm not surprised. So the cellars have stayed locked. The Colonel says they'll get a bottle

158

each on their next payday, to drink to his health, and that will be all."

"Oho," said Kate, suddenly recalling the key Maxi had given her. She'd forgotten all about it, and it was still in her jeans pocket. A thought occurred to her, and she changed the subject.

"How do you get on with the other soldiers, Willi? I saw the Colonel giving you a hard time a few days ago."

"Well, I'm the new recruit, gracious young lady. And I admit, I'm not all that smart. It takes time for things to sink in with me. So they do make fun of me a bit. They'll accept me in the end, I daresay, but maybe not until I'm a bit older or there's a newer recruit. At least, I've had a bit of luck in getting *this* job, guarding you."

Willi smiled his tentative smile.

"I expect the Colonel knows he can trust me," he said. "There's some that he wouldn't care to put in charge of a beautiful young lady." He blushed. "Of course," he went on, "you wouldn't know what I mean, having been brought up ladylike."

"I think I might guess," said Kate.

Willi blushed more deeply. "For me," he said earnestly, "it's a privilege to be here." Kate was surprised by the look of devotion in his eyes. She turned away, to spare them both embarrassment.

Willi fell asleep before Kate did. He sat with his back to the door and his snores rasping out like a saw cutting

159

into a tree trunk. Kate turned off the lights and lay quietly on her bed. She didn't think she could possibly get to sleep amid such noise and with so much to think about, but finally she did doze off. She was still fully clothed.

She was awakened by a touch on the cheek, and shot up in alarm to a sitting position. Somebody was stooping over her. In the dark she couldn't see who it was, but a voice spoke to her in a barely audible whisper. "Kate! It's Anni!"

"Anni!" Kate's whisper was equally soft, and full of wonder.

"Come with me. Quiet! Can you see?"

"Not much."

"You'll get used to it. Ssssh!"

Willi stirred, and his snoring altered its note. Both girls stood still and silent for a minute. Then Anni took Kate's hand and led her to the wardrobe in the corner of the room. Kate's eyes were getting accustomed to the dark. She could just see Anni burrowing soundlessly among hanging clothes. Anni disappeared briefly from view; then a hand reached out from between two garments and drew Kate after it. She realized she was being led into a secret passage: probably the one along which Anni had taken her to watch the guests arriving for the reception.

Anni left Kate for a moment while she closed the door of the wardrobe and a panel in the back of it; then she shone a flashlight to show the way. After a few yards the passage ceased to be pitch-black; moonlight was coming in through a tiny slit window. Anni doused the light and shone it again when they were past the opening. They picked their way over rubble lying in the narrow passageway. Anni switched off the light again at the next window and at the one after that; and then, ahead of them, they heard the sound of voices.

"Oh, the fools!" hissed Anni. She quickened her pace and positively ran along the dark, narrow passage. Kate followed as best she could. Ahead of her she heard Anni cry, "Be quiet!" Then Kate stumbled into a tiny, narrow chamber, set no doubt in one of the many mysterious recesses of the castle. The secret passage led on out the other end of it.

Here in the little chamber were George and Sonia. They seemed to have been arguing. Now, however, both were silent. George hurried over to Kate and took her in his arms.

"Oh, Kate, Kate!" he said. "Oh, am I glad to see you!" He kissed her on the lips, again and again. It was startling, as George hadn't ventured any such intimacy before. But it was quite enjoyable, and the relief of being with George was tremendous. She found herself kissing him back, in a friendly way.

"Old Schweiner needn't think he can keep *me* locked in my room," Anni said to Kate. "I've been getting out through the secret passages since I was *so* high. And I knew you'd need George. So I went into town to find him."

"And she found me with him," Sonia said. "There

161

is opposition to the pig Schweiner, especially in the university. I had hoped your friend George would join us. But I have no patience with him. He is a mere press lackey. He will not understand that it is his duty to rise up and fight oppression."

"I keep telling you, Sonia," said George, "that it's a journalist's job to report the news, not to make it!"

"And I keep telling *you*," retorted Sonia, her voice rising excitedly, "that this is a time for action, not for feeble bourgeois scruples!"

"Be quiet!" Anni repeated.

George said, "Kate, I'm going to get you out of here. I have to come back to cover the story, but I'll see you to the Serenian border. And we've got to go at once. They might find any moment that you're missing."

Anni said, "That's right. And you must be in Serenia by dawn. Do you still have the rented car, George?"

"Yes, it's at Frau Schmidt's."

"Let's see—it will take you fifteen minutes to get there, and you'll have to evade the guards on the bridge. And you mustn't take the main road to Serenia—you'd be caught at the frontier post, if not before." Anni paused and considered. "I know of one road—not much more than a track—that crosses the frontier at an unguarded point. But whether you could find it is a different question." Then she smiled brilliantly and added, "Unless I come with you!"

"You!"

"Why not? What is there for me in Essenheim? I

don't want to be a Princess, I just want to be a teenager before it's too late. I can find Uncle Ferdy in Serenia and get some money. Then off to London to join my friend Betsy!"

"Anni," said Kate, "didn't anyone tell you? The old Prince isn't in Serenia. Schweiner changed his mind. He's still being held in the castle!"

Anni exclaimed fiercely in Essenheimisch. Sonia said, "Anyway, would you go off and leave the fascist pig Schweiner in control? That is truly royal, to run away! We must have another revolution and throw the bastard out!"

Anni ignored Sonia and said, "Kate, I didn't know they still had Uncle Ferdy. I can't escape and leave him behind." Suddenly her self-possession seemed to be crumbling, and she spoke to Kate as if appealing to an older sister: "Kate, what shall we do?"

"*I* can't go and leave your uncle a prisoner, either!" said Kate firmly.

George said, "Kate, your staying here isn't going to help the old Prince. The best thing is for you and Anni to get away. I'll give you a story you can phone through to the paper from Serenia. Believe me, the only thing you can do for Prince Ferdinand is to let the world know he's been imprisoned."

Kate said, "George, you can understand plain English. I am not, repeat *not*, leaving Essenheim until Prince Ferdinand is free!"

Anni reached out for Kate's hand. "I'm staying, too," she said.

163

"There you are!" said Sonia scornfully to George. "As always, the women have the guts, the so-called man is a flinching coward!"

"What do you propose, Sonia?" George inquired mildly.

"We will overthrow Schweiner, of course! Then the royals can leave Essenheim, and good riddance! It is simple!"

"And who is going to defeat Schweiner's soldiers?"

"The students, of course!" said Sonia. "What are students for? It will be their hour of glory. They will serve the people at last!"

"The soldiers have *guns*," said George. "What do the students have?"

"They have their schlagfuss sticks and their courage."

"I'm afraid," said George, "that schlagfuss sticks and courage don't give much protection against bullets. You're not realistic, Sonia! If the soldiers are loyal to Schweiner, there's no way they can be overthrown!"

"I wonder," said Kate. "Listen to me. I've got an idea."

"It's a mad scheme!" George said ten minutes later. "And far too risky. I can't let you try it, Kate."

"You can't stop me," said Kate.

"That's right," said Sonia. "We women stick together. We are sisters. We are invincible!"

"As for you, George," said Kate. "You can get back to your car and run Sonia up to the university. Then you'll be on the spot when things start happening."

164

George sighed deeply. "All right," he said. "Some fathers have dreadful daughters. I shall tell Edward so when I see him, if I ever do. Anyway, Kate, when your crackbrained plan fails, I hope you'll get another chance to escape. I'll still be in Essenheim, waiting for you. I won't let you down."

"I know you won't," said Kate. This time it was she who put her arms around George. A minute later he went off with Sonia along the other passage, and Kate followed Anni back the way they'd come. She had a dreadful feeling that George was right to call her plan crackbrained. "Heaven help Essenheim!" she said to herself. "Heaven help us all!"

21

―――――― ◄《 》► ――――――

"Good morning, Willi!" said Kate.

The guard rubbed his eyes. "Good morning, gracious young lady," he said.

"Sorry to disturb you, Willi, but I thought it was time you were awake. The other guard will be coming to relieve you soon, won't he?"

"Yes. Thank you very much, gracious young lady. Ludwig would probably have reported me for sleeping on duty."

The look of devotion was on Willi's face again. A minute later the other guard came in with Kate's breakfast. He scowled at her and jerked a thumb at Willi.

"Off you go, rookie!" he said. "Don't fall over yourself!"

The day dragged on. It was hot and seemed extremely long. Kate managed to doze a little after lunch. She was awakened by sounds of drilling outside her window. There was obviously still a great deal of the Top Sergeant in Colonel Hermann Schweiner. He was exercising his men on the double in the sweltering heat. The sweat poured from their faces; it seemed they were being given a harder time than ever.

"They'll be thirsty after that!" Kate said to Ludwig. He hadn't stirred from his post at the door, but he couldn't have helped hearing Schweiner's barked commands.

"They're not the only ones," he grunted. "It's thirsty weather."

"Would you like a drink of water?"

"I'm not thirsty for water."

"There's nothing else in here," Kate said. The guard grunted once more.

Sounds of drilling continued to float in from outside for some time. But eventually it seemed that even Schweiner had had enough, and Kate heard the men being dismissed. The long afternoon dragged on. Kate dozed a little more. Then at six o'clock Willi reappeared, carrying her supper on a tray. Ludwig went out without a word to either of them.

Kate ate her meal, though rising excitement and apprehension had affected her stomach and it was hard to get the food down. "Were you out drilling today, Willi?" she asked.

"No, gracious young lady. This is my duty at present. When I'm not in here, I'm supposed to be having my sleeping time."

"You must need a lot of sleep, Willi," Kate remarked.

Willi blushed and then said, "The Colonel really did put them through it today. They were all a bit fed up when they came in. And they weren't any nicer to me for having escaped it, I can tell you!"

"Would you like to make yourself more popular with them?" Kate asked.

"Course I would, gracious young lady. But how?"

"Well . . ." Kate went to the wardrobe, took out her jeans, and felt in the pocket. The key was still there. Willi's eyes, round and wide, followed it as she brought it across the room.

"What is it, gracious young lady?"

"It's a key to the basement. To the wine cellars."

Willi gasped. "Fancy you having that!"

"What if I gave you this key, Willi? Then you could let the men into the cellars. They'd think differently of you then, wouldn't they? You'd make lots of friends."

"Gracious young lady!" For a moment Willi's eyes shone. Then his face clouded over. "I wouldn't dare!" he said. "They'd all get drunk as lords and the Colonel would be furious and the truth would come out, and I don't know *what* he'd do to me then!" Willi shuddered at the thought.

Kate was dismayed. She'd persuaded herself that he would accept the key with alacrity—her plan depended on it. It looked as though she'd failed. Then the door burst open and the other guard, Ludwig, came in.

"You, rookie!" he said. "I'm taking over for a while. The lads want to see you in the barrack room!"

"W-what for?" stammered Willi.

"You'll soon see! They felt sorry for you, missing this afternoon's drill. Thought you ought to have something to compensate!" There was a malicious grin on Ludwig's sour, swarthy face.

"B-but . . . the Colonel himself told me not to report for drill today. Because of being night guard for the gracious young lady."

"Well, your pals think you really need that drill, Willi. So you go along to the barrack room. I'll keep an eye on the gracious young lady."

"Are they going to beat Willi up?" Kate asked in alarm.

"No. Just a bit of fun."

It didn't seem from Willi's expression that he expected it to be fun for him. "I'm on duty, Ludwig," he said. "I can't go without permission!"

"Oh, yes, you can!" said Ludwig. "And the Colonel wouldn't mind if he did know. Come in, fellows!"

Two other grinning soldiers appeared. They seized the protesting Willi by the arms and tried to drag him away. Kate saw her chance. She began gently tossing the key from hand to hand.

"What's that?" Ludwig demanded.

"Wouldn't you like to know?"

"It looks like a castle key to me. You've no business having keys. Where is it for?"

"I'm not telling."

The other two men, still holding Willi's arms, stopped struggling with him and watched with interest. Ludwig said, "You'll tell me what that key is for. And hand it over!"

Kate said with pretended reluctance, "I won't."

Ludwig made a grab for the key. Kate held it out of his reach.

"You can't have it," she said. "It's the key to the

169

cellars. I'm keeping it until I can give it back to Maxi."

Ludwig made another grab, and this time got possession.

One of the other men said, "The cellar key! Do you think it really is?"

"We'll soon find out!" said Ludwig. "Let that fool go, and come on!"

A moment later, Kate and Willi were once more alone in the room. Willi looked apprehensive.

"If our chaps get at the drink . . ." he said.

"Yes, Willi? What?"

"Well, there's no telling, gracious young lady, there really isn't."

"It's not your fault, is it, Willi?" Kate said. "You've had nothing to do with it." She looked at her watch, wondering if time was on her side. "Do they drink fast, Willi?"

"If the drink's free," said Willi, "it'll go down faster than your eye could follow."

Silence fell between them as they contemplated, from different viewpoints, the likely consequences.

At eight o'clock promptly, Colonel Schweiner entered the room. He was resplendent in a magnificent new purple uniform, the chest of which was largely hidden by medal ribbons. As before, he dismissed Willi brusquely. Then he turned to Kate with his ingratiating smirk. "Well, gracious young lady?" he said. "Well, *Kate*? Have you now thought about your future prospects?"

"I've thought about nothing else," said Kate.

"And have you arrived at a conclusion?"

170

"Not quite."

"Not quite?" Schweiner seemed surprised. "I don't understand you. How can you still hesitate?" He put an arm around her waist. Kate managed not to recoil. Her task now was to resist Schweiner, yet at the same time convince him that victory was at hand if he went on trying. And she had to keep him trying for as long as possible.

"Oh, Colonel, you shouldn't!" she protested, giving him a sideways glance that strongly hinted that he should. Schweiner, encouraged, planted a slobbery kiss on her cheek.

"Colonel! How dare you?" Kate cried with simulated indignation. She wondered if she could give herself the pleasure of slapping his face, but decided that that was more than she could get away with.

Schweiner unbuttoned his purple jacket and took off his gun belt. "Kate! Dear Kate! Accept me and you shall be the wife—the lawful wife—of Schweiner. Of Hermann Schweiner himself! There shall be a double wedding: you and me; Rudi and Elsa."

This prospect didn't appeal to Kate a bit. She steeled herself to keep the game going. Eventually Schweiner, with both arms clamped around her, was kissing such parts of her face and neck as he could get at, while with some difficulty she kept her mouth away from him. The smell of his breath—garlic sausage, at a guess—assisted her in this endeavor.

"Dearest Kate, say yes to me!" Schweiner urged, in a hoarse rasp that was the nearest he could get to an amorous whisper.

171

Kate disengaged herself. "Give me just one more minute!" she begged. "It is such an important step, I must try to think coolly."

"Of course, my sweet. But please, Kate, think quickly as well. I have many duties and cannot stay much longer."

Kate went to the window, moving slowly and absent-mindedly, as if deep in thought. And when she looked out, her heart leaped up and it was all she could do not to cheer. A posse of students was proceeding in a straggling column up the narrow service road that led to the castle's side entrance. It was led by Klaus Klappdorf, Sonia, and Aleksi, marching side by side. Many of the students were carrying schlagfuss sticks; most of the rest had homemade weapons of one kind or another. And, thank goodness, somebody must have impressed on them the need for silence. They weren't making a sound.

At that moment, however, sounds were heard inside the castle. Loud, drunken voices; laughter; a crash as of something being broken. Schweiner cried, "What's that?" and took four or five paces toward the door. Before he could reach it, the door burst open. The two soldiers who had earlier been with Ludwig reeled into the room. Both were carrying bottles. Schweiner recoiled a step. They were too drunk to be afraid of him.

"Have a drink, Shargeant!" said one, waving his bottle and spilling wine down Schweiner's immaculate new uniform.

"He'sh not a Shargeant now, he'sh a Colonel!" the other pointed out.

"It doeshn't make any difference! He'sh shtill good old Shargeant Schweiner! Drink, Shargeant, drink! And you too, gracious young lady!"

Willi peered in from the doorway, terrified. From beyond him more raised, raucous voices could be heard. Schweiner, outraged, roared a fierce Essenheimisch oath and buffeted each of the two drunken men in turn. One of them fell straight to the floor; the other staggered in a circle and then fell on top of his friend. Schweiner kicked them both.

Then other sounds were heard: shots, shouting, a bellow of pain, a rush of feet. Schweiner swung round to face the door. Through it surged a mass of people: Klaus Klappdorf, Sonia, half a dozen students. Schweiner dived for his gun belt, which lay on Kate's bed; but Kate was quicker and had thrown herself on top of it. Schweiner turned, hurled himself at Klaus, and tripped over one of the fallen soldiers. A student caught him off balance and sent him crashing to the ground on his back in a corner of the room. Two others grabbed him and held him down.

"Great!" said Klaus. "Now, what'll we do with him?"

Just then, a clear, commanding voice was heard: "Let me through, please! Let me through!" Two or three students stood aside. It was Rudi, still in his officer's uniform. He drew his revolver and pointed it at the struggling Schweiner.

"Let him go, fellows!" he ordered. "I have him cov-

173

ered. Hermann Schweiner, you are under arrest!"

Schweiner, released, rose ponderously to his feet. Rudi said quietly, "Make one more move and you're a dead man."

Other people were filtering into the room now. One of them was Anni; another was George, who seemed not merely to have followed the story but to have caught up with it.

Rudi called, "Maxi! Maxi! Where's Maxi?" The shout was taken up in the doorway and echoed along the corridor outside: "Maxi! Maxi!" Schweiner half stood, half crouched in his corner, breathing hard; the gun was still on him. More people crowded into the doorway. The jailer appeared, pushing his way between them and carrying handcuffs. But he could hardly bring himself to go within arm's length of Schweiner.

Rudi, speaking quietly again, said, "Schweiner, put your wrists together in front of you." Gingerly, Maxi put the handcuffs on him. And Schweiner seemed deflated to two-thirds of his former size by this action.

"Take him to the cells," Rudi said. A little knot of students helped Maxi bundle Schweiner away; others dragged the two drunken soldiers from the room. The crowd gradually thinned out.

"Well, that's that," said Klaus with satisfaction. "It's all over but the shouting. Our people took the soldiers by surprise and they were too drunk to resist. Only a few shots fired, and nobody hurt that I know of. Now," he added, "we'll adjourn to the Prime Minister's office to decide what happens next."

"Is that necessary?" Rudi asked lightly. "We've restored the position. I as Prince Laureate will simply take up where I left off on Thursday night."

"Restored the position?" said Sonia. "Prince Laureate? Who says there is to be a Prince Laureate?"

Rudi looked from her to Klaus. "Well, Rudi," Klaus said in a conciliatory tone, "the old Prince has abdicated, Stockhausen's vanished, and Schweiner's in the cells. It does look rather as though it's time for a new start."

"I'll *give* you a new start," said Rudi with a touch of impatience. "That's been my intention all along. Don't worry about it, just leave it to me."

There was a brief silence, broken only by distant cheers and shouting from the direction of the dungeons.

"I don't think you quite understand, Rudi," said Klaus. "The students are in control. It is up to them to decide what happens next."

For a moment there was anger in Rudi's face. Then Kate, watching attentively, could see it being brought under control. "Very well," he said. "I will meet you, and any students who wish to come, in Dr. Stockhausen's office in half an hour's time."

22

Dusk in Essenheim; lights going on in the castle. In the big comfortable office that had once been Dr. Stockhausen's, Sonia was taking charge of the meeting. She sat on the former Prime Minister's desk while students squatted around her on the floor.

Kate, George, and Anni, none of whom had been specifically invited, sat discreetly and unobtrusively at the back. Sounds of roistering still floated up from below. Most of the soldiers, helplessly drunk, had been driven by students with schlagfuss sticks into the dungeons, though a few had managed to discard their Army jackets and join their conquerors. Now the schlagfuss players in turn were helping themselves to the contents of the castle cellars. At least the students who had come to the meeting looked fairly sober, Kate observed.

Now Klaus and Rudi entered, both smiling. Rudi had changed from his Army officer's uniform to a T-shirt and jeans. He and Klaus took chairs at either side of Sonia, and she opened the proceedings.

"Fellow members of the proletariat!" she began.

"The people have come to power in Essenheim. The degenerate effete aristocratic Prince and the fascist tyrant Schweiner have in turn been overthrown. I propose that we now establish a revolutionary government."

"Seconded," Rudi said cheerfully.

Sonia stared. *"You!"* she said. "You, seconding *this*? What sort of revolutionary are *you*?"

"I have resigned my Princedom. I am Rudolf Hohlberg, ordinary citizen and man of the people."

"I do not accept you as one of us," said Sonia.

Klaus intervened. "Mr. Hohlberg has the same rights as any other citizen," he contended. "That's so, isn't it, friends?"

There was general agreement with Klaus's view. Sonia looked angry but made no further objection. "Very well. Does anyone oppose my resolution?" she asked.

Nobody did. It was carried with acclaim.

"Next we need a title for the regime!" said Sonia.

"The People's Republic of Essenheim," Rudi suggested promptly.

" 'People' is too general," objected a black-bearded young man. "This is *our* scene. Let's make it the *Young People's* Republic of Essenheim."

This was unanimously approved.

"Now," Sonia continued, "we require a President. Would anyone like to submit a nomination?"

She looked expectantly round the gathering. Somebody obligingly said, "I would like to nominate Sonia Zackendorf."

177

"Are there any other nominations?" Sonia asked; and then, very rapidly: "No? In that case I reluctantly accept—"

But she wasn't quite quick enough. A girl with long blond hair sprang up and said, "I nominate Rudi Hohlberg."

Sonia asked unbelievingly, "You would nominate this degenerate ex-Princeling?"

"Yes, please," said the blond-haired girl. There were sighs of assent from several other female students. A dark girl at the back said, "I saw him arrest Colonel Schweiner. It was *marvelous*. Just like the movies!"

"We'd better take a vote!" said Sonia crossly. There was a show of hands. Sonia declared herself to have been elected. But it was obvious to everyone in the room that Rudi, collecting the entire feminine vote, had in fact won a clear majority.

"I think you've accidentally miscounted, Sonia," said Klaus with tact. "Hadn't we better try again?" And after a second show of hands, which was equally decisive, Sonia gave way more or less gracefully.

"Congratulations, Comrade Hohlberg," she said, in a tone of voice suggesting that she would gladly have seen him boiled in oil. "You are the first President of the Young People's Republic of Essenheim."

During the next half hour a succession of ministries was distributed. By way of conciliating Sonia, Rudi proposed her as Prime Minister, and she was elected unopposed. Klaus was elected Minister of Defense, in which capacity he sent a message down to the schlagfuss play-

178

ers in the cellars, conveying the grateful thanks of their country. Werner, the black-bearded student, became Minister of Information and was dispatched to the radio station to see that Moritz read out a suitable bulletin.

Aleksi was appointed Minister of Culture, in which capacity he announced his intention of producing a revised version, taking into account the fact that the Essenheim flag was purple, of "The Red Flag." This project, combining revolution with national feeling, was warmly welcomed. Finally Rudi announced that the Cabinet would meet at nine the next morning, and adjourned the meeting.

"High time too," remarked a student just in front of Kate. "Now we can *all* go down to the cellars. Why should the schlagfuss thugs have all the fun?" They trooped out with alacrity.

Kate and George went up to the front of the room, and George attempted to use the telephone on Dr. Stockhausen's desk, but pulled a face and reported, "Still no outgoing calls. I haven't been able to get through to London since Wednesday." Then he, Kate, and Rudi headed toward the private apartments. Anni seemed to have slipped quietly away.

"Well, Mr. President," said George in a faintly ironic tone, "are you satisfied with tonight's proceedings?"

"Oh, it was all a lot of nonsense," said Rudi cheerfully. "If I were you, George, I wouldn't be in any hurry to get my story through to London."

"What do you mean?"

"Well, they're only playing at being a government. It can't last, you know. There'll have to be a proper

179

regime that can take charge and that really means business."

"And how is that going to come about?"

"We'll have to wait and see."

"What about freeing your uncle, Rudi?" asked Kate.

"I'll see about that tomorrow. We can't release the poor old boy into all the turmoil there is down there at present. And now, Kate, here we are at your room. I suggest you lock your door on the inside, just in case of intrusive drunks, and go peacefully to sleep."

"And I'd better go back to Frau Schmidt's," said George, "or she'll be locking me out."

Kate was left on her own. She didn't think she'd be able to sleep. She switched on the radio. Moritz was explaining in tones of happy excitement that it was another great day in the history of Essenheim, the first day of the Young People's Republic; also that Quick 'n' Safe Sure-Fire Superstar Elixir would cure everybody's ailments and that you could buy a good used car very cheaply at Willi Bamberger's lot, just behind the Town Hall. And then it was pop records again. Kate switched off, and the exertions of the past twenty-four hours had their effect on her. She was soon fast asleep.

When Kate woke the next morning, the private apartments of Essenheim Castle were an empty world. The doors of Prince Ferdinand's, Rudi's, and Anni's rooms were all open, and the beds had not been slept in. No staff was to be seen; no table was laid in breakfast room or dining room.

Leaving the private rooms, Kate wandered through the Great Hall and found twenty or thirty students asleep, fully dressed, on the floor. Some were snoring, some twisting and turning restlessly, some simply flat out. Clearly it was the morning after the night before. In the castle kitchens there was again no staff, but a handful of students, most of them only half awake, were foraging for breakfast. Someone had succeeded in making coffee, and without a word or a smile pushed a cup across to Kate. A reek of alcohol floated up from the cellars, but there wasn't a sound. Probably there were people sleeping down there as well. Kate didn't feel like exploring. She did, however, want desperately to find Rudi and to secure the old Prince's release and a flight out of the country.

Recalling the Cabinet meeting, now due to start, she pulled herself together and set off briskly for the Prime Minister's office in the other wing. Here, surely, she'd be able to get hold of Rudi. And here she found people up and alert, and Sonia looking in irritation at her watch. Klaus was present, and so were most of the other members of the Cabinet elected last night, but Rudi hadn't arrived.

Twenty minutes passed. Sonia said crossly, "I knew all along he was a playboy. Rudi Hohlberg, man of the people, indeed! He is still the effete aristocrat. Probably he is waiting for someone to take him his breakfast in bed. We will start without him."

She took her seat on Dr. Stockhausen's desk and rapped on it for silence. Conversation died down. And then suddenly there was the sound of heavy, regular

181

footsteps. The door of the Prime Minister's office flew open. Two big solid men with very short hair, wearing clean, pressed blue-gray uniforms and with guns at their hips, strode into the room.

"I thought so! There're more of them in here!" said one to the other; and then, in a peremptory tone: "Come on, out! This way!"

"This is a Cabinet meeting," said Sonia with dignity. "It is strictly private. Please leave the room at once, whoever you are."

The men didn't trouble to reply. Roughly they herded everyone together, shoving or cuffing those who didn't move fast enough, and forced them out the door. Kate found herself being hurried along with a group of people that included Klaus, Aleksi, Sonia, and nine or ten students.

They were driven through the Great Hall, from which the sleeping students had now been cleared, and down the stone steps into the reeking dungeons. Kate tried to speak to one of the men, but he took no notice of her and continued urging the little group along. Cell after cell after cell was now occupied, and from some of them people were shouting. At length they came to a run of empty cells into which they were thrust, one at a time, with contemptuous indifference. Kate's door was slammed and locked, and the captors walked away. She was imprisoned in the dungeons of Essenheim.

23

It was the worst and longest day of Kate's life. She didn't know who her captors were, and there was no one she could ask. From somewhere along the line she could hear Sonia yelling imprecations, among which the words "fascist" and "pig" could be distinguished, but this told her little—in Sonia's vocabulary it might have meant anybody. Occasionally a uniformed man, gun in holster, would stride along the passage, his progress marked by a wave of appeals and complaints from cell after cell as he went by; but no such guard ever stopped or said a word. The only food was a bowl of greasy, gristly stew, which Kate could not touch.

She didn't cry, though she felt like doing so. She kept despair at bay by telling herself a hundred times that this imprisonment couldn't last long. And she was right. Toward nightfall—though nightfall in itself meant nothing, for the only light she had seen all day was that of a feeble electric bulb—she heard two sets of heavy, echoing footsteps approaching along the passage. The door of her cell was flung open. A guard

183

with insignia of rank on his shoulder strode in. "You are the girl from London?" he inquired brusquely.

"Yes," said Kate.

"You are to be released. Follow me."

"But . . . who *are* you?"

"That is not your concern."

"I mean, what's your organization? Who imprisoned me? Who says I'm to be let out?"

"I am head of the Finkel Industries Security Service. The order for your release comes from Herr Finkel himself. That is all I know. This way, please."

Kate was taken back to her own room.

"You are free within the castle," the guard said. "You will not be allowed to leave it without Herr Finkel's permission."

Once more Kate was left alone. She had hardly had time to look around when the telephone rang. The voice was Rudi's.

"Kate!" he said. "So you're safe in your room. Thank goodness for that! Please stay where you are. I'll see you in the morning."

"Rudi! What's this all about?"

"Never mind, Kate. Don't worry. Go to bed. Sleep well."

"But Rudi . . . Rudi! *Rudi!* . . . Are you still there?"

It was no use. He had hung up. And when she tried to put through a call to London, an operator's voice said, "No outgoing calls at present!"

After a confusion of dreams involving soldiers, students, Schweiner, guards, passages, and cells, Kate was

184

caught up in a nightmare of being imprisoned for life. She woke in perspiring panic and couldn't sleep again for hours. It was daylight before she drifted into a more peaceful half sleep, from which she was awakened by a chinking of china. The maid Lilli was at her bedside with a tray of coffee, rolls, butter, and honey.

"Lilli!" said Kate. "I haven't seen you in days!"

"No, gracious young lady. We were frightened by the gunshots and all went home. But this morning I was telephoned and told to come in as usual. And everything seems normal, except"— her voice still sounded uncertain—"except for all those people in the cells. Anyway, a few minutes ago I saw Prince Rudi and he said, 'Lilli, take coffee and rolls to Fräulein Kate.' So here I am." She dropped a curtsey and went out.

As she ate, Kate turned the radio on. It was the usual, invariable pop music. Then a pause, the sounding of the door chime, and the voice of Moritz. "Well, folks," he began, "here we are on Day Two of the return to law and order. For those of you who missed the earlier bulletins, Essenheim has firm government once more. You'll be delighted to know that the new Prime Minister is our leading citizen, Herr Konrad Finkel, proprietor of Finkel's Wineries, the Finkel Bank, the Finkel Mortgage Corporation, Amalgamated Finkel Industries, and United Finkel International. Don't take time out to rejoice; just go about your work as usual in a clean, sober, responsible, and obedient manner." Moritz paused. "And remember, folks, that whatever happens you can still rely on Quick 'n' Safe Sure-Fire Superstar Elixir. It's a Finkel product. . . ."

Kate switched the radio off, dressed, and hurried from her room. Just outside the doorway she bumped into Rudi. In contrast to the period dress of Thursday, the Army uniform of Friday, and the T-shirt and jeans of Saturday, his attire now was a neat white shirt and tie and a dark business suit. He held her by the shoulders and kissed her affectionately.

"Congratulate me, Kate," he said. "After a few hours as President I am now once more Prince Laureate."

"But . . . I can't keep up with it, Rudi. What's happened since Saturday night?"

Rudi gave a shrug. "It's quite simple. There's been another revolution. Herr Finkel has taken over. I must say, I think his government will be much more stable than that of the students ever would have been."

"And he's letting you keep the title of Prince Laureate?"

"Yes."

"And what about Elsa Schweiner? I suppose you won't be marrying her after all."

"No, indeed. That is all off."

"Does Herr Finkel have a daughter for you to be engaged to?"

"You are too cynical, Kate. Herr Finkel has no daughter. But he has what was needed yesterday. He has the security staff who collect the produce from the peasants and the interest on his mortgages."

"His heavies, you mean? His strong-arm squad? I heard about them from the Mayor."

"Call them that if you wish, Kate. They were far

more than a match for the ridiculous students and their schlagfuss sticks. It was all over in a matter of minutes."

"I know that," said Kate. "And I spent a day in the cells."

"I'm sorry about that. It took me all day to work myself sufficiently into Finkel's favor to secure your release and my own restoration as Prince Laureate. He was inclined to be distrustful of me at first."

"You can't blame him for that," said Kate. "Where's George?"

"George has not been seen since the Finkel takeover was announced. Stockhausen and Cousin Friedrich are still missing, too. Apart from that, everything is under control. Some of the soldiers have been sworn in again, and are now at the service of the new regime. Those who refused are still in the dungeons. The students will cool their heels there, too, for a few days, and then be sent back to the university."

"That's great!" said Kate sardonically. "And you get to be Prince Laureate under Herr Finkel! You'll have to do what he tells you, won't you?"

"There will be no difficulty, Kate. Herr Finkel and I see eye to eye. Come, you must renew acquaintance with him. He is anxious to see and reassure you."

The outer office of the Prime Minister's suite was now guarded by a massively built man in the uniform of the Finkel Industries Security Service. He sprang to attention and saluted smartly as Rudi approached. In the office two neatly suited male clerks and a typist in a navy-blue costume and white silk shirt were hard at work. Rudi and Kate went into the inner sanctum.

Herr Finkel, as immaculate as when Kate had seen him before, sat at the enormous desk that had been Dr. Stockhausen's. He rose to his feet and bowed punctiliously.

"Good morning, Prince," he said. "Good morning, gracious young lady."

"Good morning, Prime Minister," said Rudi with equal formality.

"I must apologize, gracious young lady," Herr Finkel said, "for your ordeal yesterday. It resulted from failure at a low level of command to make a necessary distinction."

"Oh," said Kate. She wasn't inclined to be too forgiving, after the dreadful day she'd had. But Herr Finkel didn't wait for her to comment further. "I am glad to tell you," he went on, "that after the unfortunate events of the past few days we have now mastered the situation and are ready to make progress. The Prince and I together will lead Essenheim into the twentieth century."

"Are you quite sure there won't be another revolution tomorrow?" asked Kate.

"Revolutions are no joke, gracious young lady," said Herr Finkel coldly. "We want no more such nonsense here. Calm, order, and stability are what we require, and an atmosphere in which business can flourish."

"Especially," added Rudi, "such progressive businesses as those of Herr Finkel."

Kate recalled the Mayor's unfavorable comments about Herr Finkel and his enterprises. "What do the ordinary people think about all this?" she asked.

"The ordinary people?" Herr Finkel stared. "What has it to do with them?"

"Well . . . I suppose they do live here."

"Yes," said Herr Finkel. "They live here. They have their function. They till the land, keep the little shops, perform their menial duties. That is all I require of them. And if they behave themselves I shall see that they are well fed and housed. Just as a wise farmer looks after his animals, so a wise government will look after its common people. But the animals do not run the farm, nor should the common people run the government."

Herr Finkel gave Kate his wintry little smile.

"Now, my dear young lady," he said, "why do you suppose that, on the first day of my Prime Ministership, with a hundred urgent matters requiring my attention, I am receiving you here and have given instructions that we are not to be disturbed?"

"I haven't the least idea," said Kate.

"I have come to a decision," said Herr Finkel. "Or rather, the Prince and I have come to a decision. It is that the Prince should marry as soon as possible."

"That," said Kate decisively, "has nothing to do with me."

"Don't be so sure, gracious young lady. Suppose the Prince were to marry *you*? By that I mean, suppose he were actually to *marry* you?"

Kate gasped. "What about Princess Etta?" she asked faintly.

"Princess Etta is no problem. Her wealth and title are not important to me. Her family will find her another match. I am more anxious that the Prince should marry soon than that he should marry royalty."

"Kate, dear," said Rudi with an air of great sincerity, "I love you. I have loved you since the day I first saw you at that party in London. My uncle thought marriage with a commoner was impossible, but Herr Finkel sees no such objection. Isn't that splendid? Our happiness is assured."

Kate looked into his face. In spite of all the events of the past few days, she almost believed him.

"Say you will have me, Kate," Rudi said softly. "Say you love me."

Kate felt the words "Yes, Rudi" rising to her lips. Her sense of self-preservation struggled for survival. She swallowed twice, then said defensively, "Isn't this rather *public* for a proposal?"

"Gracious young lady," said Herr Finkel, "I strongly advise you to accept. Marriage, I must remind you, is the most serious business transaction in life. You now have a highly advantageous opportunity."

Kate was silent. Herr Finkel went on, "No doubt you think of Essenheim as a small and backward country. Let me assure you that the Prince and I have far-reaching plans for its future. Ours will be a truly businesslike regime. We aim to develop Essenheim into a center for worldwide tax avoidance. And we shall of course encourage tourism, issue postage stamps . . ."

"We could have a royal wedding issue!" Rudi exclaimed enthusiastically. "How would you like that, Kate? A stamp with a picture of you and me on it!"

Kate was silent. Her sense of self-preservation was

recovering from the shock of Rudi's proposal. She felt she was suffering from a surfeit of honorable intentions: first Schweiner's, now his.

"You hesitate, my dear young lady," said Herr Finkel. "Well, take your time. But not too much of it. Perhaps, Prince, you should continue the conversation with Fräulein Kate in private, and leave me to grapple with the affairs of state."

24

———— ◄❮ ❯► ————

"I'm tired of all this," Kate told Rudi when they'd left the Prime Minister's room. "*Please* understand. I want to go home. And what about your uncle? Where is he now?"

"Ah, yes, my uncle. I had almost forgotten him."

"*Forgotten* him?"

"Forgive me, Kate. So much has happened in the past few days. . . . I suppose Uncle Ferdy must still be in the dungeons, where Schweiner put him."

"Oh, no!" cried Kate. "Can't we get him out?"

"Well," said Rudi doubtfully, "I suppose we can try."

He led the way to the dungeons. As they went down the stone steps, their noses were assaulted by a strong smell of disinfectant and their ears by shouts, groans, and mutterings from several directions. Half a dozen women with scrubbing brushes and galvanized buckets were swabbing the stone floors. In charge of them was massive, muscular Bertha, the jailer's wife.

"Good morning, Bertha," said Rudi affably.

Bertha dropped a minimal curtsey. She did not look at all pleased. "It's not such a good morning for me,

Highness, I can tell you!" she said sourly "First the soldiers, then the students, and one lot as bad as the other. You wouldn't believe the filthy mess they've made down here! And then," she went on, dropping her voice, "there's this lot of Herr Finkel's, beating people up and kicking and locking them away. A right lot of thugs *they* are, I can tell you. In fact, Prince"— her voice was rising again—"if you want to know, I've had enough of it all and I can't stand much more, and neither can my women here!"

"There, there," said Rudi in soothing tones. "It was just a passing phase. Things are settling down, I assure you."

Rudi called to a guard to take them to the old Prince. They were led past scores of cells, now mostly occupied by soldiers or students. The soldiers were quiet, appearing to take their confinement philosophically, as a hazard of Army life, but the students had recovered from their earlier states of shock or hangover. They jeered and shouted abuse at the guards, and a few of them cheered ironically as Rudi and Kate went past.

The more important prisoners had now been put in a row of cells at the farthest remove from the steps to the outer world. Rudi and Kate looked in through the tiny barred window of each in turn. Schweiner, red-faced and sweating, intermittently bawled demands for his release and called down the wrath of heaven on those who had imprisoned the savior of the country. Sonia, in the cell next door, shrieked abuse impartially at Schweiner and at Finkel, but took time out to howl "Capitalist lackey!" at Rudi. In such lulls as arose, Aleksi plaintively recited his poem based on "Stone walls do not a prison make." He sounded rather less sure of this than on the previous occasion.

In the last cell of all, the old Prince sat on a bare bench, awake yet blank-eyed, taking no notice of anything that went on. He was clutching a threadbare blanket round his shoulders as a cloak.

"Kindly release Prince Ferdinand into my charge," said Rudi to the guard. But the man was reluctant.

"My orders are that no one gets out," he said.

Rudi drew himself up. "I am the Prince Laureate of Essenheim. Mine is the highest authority in the land. I order you to unlock this cell, and to send for some of Prince Ferdinand's clothes."

"I'll just check with the Prime Minister's office," said the guard uneasily. He hurried away along the passage.

When the guard returned, he said, "Herr Finkel says it's all right for you to see the Prince in the interview room for a few minutes, and afterward he can have his clothes and go to his former quarters, under guard. But he's not to be released."

Rudi frowned but said no more. The cell was unlocked, and the old Prince shambled between a couple of guards to a little room farther along the passage where he, Kate, and Rudi sat round a bare table. Here the Prince's blankness was replaced by distress, though his mind still seemed clouded.

"Rudi!" he muttered. "Little Rudi, my favorite nephew! Can you bear to see your old uncle treated like this?"

"I did not lock you up, Uncle," said Rudi. "And I

194

have been at some pains to get you released." Kate was startled by the coldness in his voice.

There were tears in the old man's eyes. Kate put her arms round him and kissed his cheek. He smiled a watery smile.

"You're a good girl," he said.

"If it pleases you to know, Uncle," said Rudi, "let me tell you that I propose to marry Kate."

"Oh!" said the Prince. The words seemed to concentrate his mind. He asked, in a brisker tone than he'd used before, "Have you accepted him, Kate?"

"No," said Kate.

"Not yet," said Rudi.

"Kate," said the old Prince, "I should be happy to have you as the mother of Rudi's heir, if I live long enough to see one. And yet, for your own sake"— he put a hand on hers—"I think you should refuse."

"It is nothing to do with you, Uncle," said Rudi.

"Prince Ferdinand—" Kate began, but the old man stopped her.

"You must call me Uncle Ferdy," he said.

"Uncle Ferdy, it's *you* I'm worrying about. What do you want to do now? Where do you want to go?"

"I want to leave Essenheim, Kate. My time here has passed. I should like best to join my married daughter at her villa in Serenia. She has staff and no children. She wouldn't mind looking after an old man. It wouldn't be for long."

"I'm sure Rudi can arrange for you to leave," Kate said comfortingly. "How soon would you like to go, Uncle Ferdy? Tomorrow?"

195

But the old man was looking vacant again. Obviously he wasn't listening.

"Uncle Ferdy!" she said. "Uncle Ferdy!"

It was no use. The old Prince's mind, or as much of it as was present, had wandered away from her. "They have much better TV reception in Serenia," he remarked. When the guard returned a minute later to take him away, he stumbled obediently along without making any protest or saying any farewells.

"Rudi," said Kate when they were left alone, "you must get him out of here before he loses his wits altogether. *Please* fix it with Herr Finkel for Uncle Ferdy and me to fly to Serenia. As soon as possible."

"I don't know whether that can be done," said Rudi. "Kate, I must warn you of another possibility. Uncle may be put on trial."

"On *trial!*" Kate was staggered. "Whatever is he supposed to have done?"

"Oh, that's neither here nor there. It would be easy to find a few charges, if Herr Finkel were so minded. Conspiring with Schweiner, perhaps."

"But that's ridiculous. Of *course* he didn't conspire with Schweiner!"

"That doesn't matter. It would be a neat way of getting both of them on the same charge. The evidence could be arranged." Rudi added with a smile, "However, Uncle Ferdy would *not* be likely to stand trial if you accepted me."

"Rudi, you can't be serious. That would be blackmail. I just don't understand. Why, I don't believe you really want to marry me at all!"

"That's where you're wrong, Kate." He tried to take her hand, but she pulled it away. "I am truly eager to do so. I'm *determined* that you shall accept me." He added, as if clinching the matter, "So is Herr Finkel!"

"Rudi," said Kate, "you are unspeakable!"

Shaken and horrified, she made her way, alone, to her own room.

25

―――――― ❧❦ ――――――

Back in her room, Kate felt something approaching despair. She was on her own again. She had seen neither George nor Anni since the day before yesterday. She had no obvious way of getting out of Essenheim, except by agreeing to marry Rudi. And the old Prince was still a prisoner.

Without much hope, she lifted the telephone receiver and said she wanted to put a call through to London. The voice of an operator said, "No outgoing calls today." Though that was what she'd expected, Kate's heart sank farther. Then the operator went on, in a confidential tone, "Is that Fräulein Kate? Yes? I have a message for you. Strictly private."

Kate waited eagerly.

"It's from Princess Anni. Pack your bag, she says, and be ready to go. And stay in your room till she comes!"

"Is that all?"

"That's all I know. I don't want to know any more."

Kate put her things together. It didn't take long. Getting her bag packed gave her a sense of progress. She sat on the bed to wait for Anni. Time went by. She walked over to the window and looked out. It was raining steadily. A couple of men in capes—presumably from Herr Finkel's security squad—patrolled the bridge that led from the castle toward the town. She went to the door and peeked down the hallway toward the old Prince's room; but it was now guarded by a ferocious-looking member of Herr Finkel's security squad, and she wouldn't have cared to go visiting anyway, in case Anni arrived. She went back to the bed, put her feet up, and after her previous uneasy night found herself nodding off to sleep.

Scrabbling sounds from the wardrobe awoke her. She sat up with a jolt, to see Anni emerging. Her face, hands, T-shirt, and jeans were smeared with black ink and her expression was joyful. She ran to embrace Kate, transferring some of the ink to Kate's own person and clothing.

"Kate!" she cried. "We've done such tremendous things. And we're all set to get you out of here!"

"Who's 'we'?" Kate asked.

"Me and George and the Mayor and Herr Beyer and Hansi. You know Hansi? He's Herr Beyer's apprentice at the printing shop. I always liked him and he always liked me and we didn't even know we liked each other because I was in the castle and he was in the town and castle and town don't mix but we did like each other all the same and now we've been doing this marvelous job together and we're going to stay together and George is great and the Mayor's great and Herr Beyer's great and *everybody's* great and I've

199

never had such fun in my life and never mind heaven helping Essenheim *we're* helping Essenheim and George will come up here as soon as they've finished and oh Kate I'm so excited!"

Kate gripped Anni's shoulders. "Anni," she said. "Tell me. One step at a time. Just *what* have you been up to?"

"It's the *Essenheim Free Press,*" Anni said. "We've really made it a free press. A special number. Unofficial. A terrific editorial. George wrote it and I translated it and Hansi set it in type and Herr Beyer printed it and the Mayor stacked the copies. And now they're distributing it all round the town. Calling all Essenheimers to meet in the marketplace this evening. And *they'll* decide what happens, not the people in the castle. And one of Herr Finkel's men heard the machines running and came to see what was going on, and you know what happened? The Mayor laid him out. *Wham! Pow!* And we locked him in the lavatory and went on printing. And the Mayor'll lead the townspeople on a march to the castle, but *we* won't be there because I've fixed it with Riverman Flusswasser for him to be waiting for us down at the quay, in the *Lorelei.* And you and I and George and Hansi will all be getting out of Essenheim together."

"But Anni," said Kate, "what about your uncle?"

"Oh, that's all right," said Anni airily. "We'll rescue *him*, too, as soon as George arrives."

"Uncle Ferdy's shut up in his own room," said Kate, "with a guard on the door. Even if we could get him past the guard, we'd *never* squeeze him through that narrow little secret passage. I only just managed to get through it myself."

"I told you, there are *lots* of passages in this castle, and I know them all. There's a nice one at the far side of the Great Hall. Just the right size for Uncle Ferdy."

"But . . . we'd have to *get* him there. That mightn't be easy."

"A day like this, I feel like I can do *anything*!" declared Anni. "It can't go wrong."

Then, suddenly, she came down to earth. "At least, I *hope* it can't," she said.

More time passed. Rain still poured down steadily. Anni went to her own room, washed, changed her clothes, and put a few of her own possessions into Kate's bag: "One bag between us is all we can take," she said. Then there was nothing they could do until George arrived. They sat on the bed together and talked a good deal about London. Anni sighed dreamily at the thought of movies, theaters, concerts, and innumerable shops. She breathed with awe the names of Harrod's and Liberty's. Kate, for her part, just wanted to be back in her semidetached home in Hammersmith.

At last, the expected sounds were heard from the wardrobe. Guided by Anni, George emerged into the room. He came straight across to Kate and kissed her. Kate kissed him back. He kissed her again. Anni said, "Hey, what about me?" George kissed Anni. Then he said, "All right, the love-in's over. Let's get going. We

201

have to rescue Prince Ferdinand. How do we do it?"

Anni said, "We have to get him out of his room and across the Great Hall. Finkel's men must be spread rather thinly; there aren't all *that* many of them. If we can lay out the one on Uncle Ferdy's door, we can probably spirit him away without any more trouble."

George said, "What weapons do we have for bashing guards?"

Anni said, "There's that vase on the window ledge. Why don't you pick it up, George, walk over to Uncle's room with us, then, while we chat up the guard, you get round behind him and—"

Kate said, "Bring it down, hard."

George said, "*Not* a reporter's job." He grinned. "But I'll try."

Anni said, "Trying's not enough. You have to *succeed*!"

The three of them walked along to the old Prince's room. George carried the heavy glass vase and Kate her bag. Outside the Prince's door, a guard challenged them. Anni said coolly, "I want to see my uncle."

The guard said, "Have you a permit?"

Anni said, "Do I need a permit to see my own uncle?"

The guard said, "My orders are that nobody goes in without a permit from the Prime Minister's office."

Anni became fluently indignant. While her verbal assault was occupying the guard's attention, George slipped around behind him and raised the vase. With an agonized expression, he brought it down with a nasty crash on the guard's head. The guard fell instantly. George looked at him with surprise and horror, as if he hadn't expected any such result, and then carefully put the vase down on the floor. Anni, with more presence of mind, pushed the Prince's door open, and they bundled the unconscious guard inside.

The Prince was in his usual chair, sitting glassy-eyed before the television set. George took one of his arms and Kate the other, and they helped him to his feet. Anni picked up Kate's bag, then darted to the door, looked out, and signaled to them to come on.

The Prince tottered between them. A servant, passing them in the corridor, gave a little bob in their direction and went on, apparently seeing nothing amiss. They moved from the private apartments down the staircase into the Great Hall. Anni went ahead, looked round, and again signaled them on; there were no guards in sight. As quickly as they could, half carrying the old man, Kate and George followed.

Then there was a burst of shouting and a thudding of many feet along the passageway that led into the Great Hall from the direction of the dungeons. And into the hall poured a mob of soldiers and students, waving guns and schlagfuss sticks respectively. They milled around aimlessly as if, newly released, they didn't know what was expected of them. But following them up, like sheep dogs with their flock, came a formidable group. They were the brawny cleaning women of the castle, and directing them was Bertha, the jailer's wife.

Kate, George, and Anni pressed their backs against the wall and watched. The Prince stared blankly, as if no sight could now make any impression on him. Guards emerged in twos and threes, running, from various directions. Rallying the vanguard of soldiers and students, Bertha pressed forward. Her shock troops, the cleaning women, moved into the lead. Some with mops and brooms at the ready, some swinging galvanized buckets around them to clear the way, they charged through the Great Hall. Bertha herself, protected by two stout lieutenants bearing trash-can lids, cut and thrust her way toward the Prime Minister's office.

Bodies swayed and jostled everywhere. Guns were useless in the crush. Uniformed Finkel guards struggled with clusters of assailants. Bertha was out of sight now, but the battle went on. For a while there was total confusion. Then Bertha came into view again, dragging a limp, unconscious Herr Finkel by the collar. A couple of guards tried to rescue him but went down in a scrum of threshing limbs.

"Come on!" urged George. "Let's get out of here, fast!"

"This way!" Anni hissed. She hurried them round the fringes of the battle to the farther side of the hall, where a dozen lifesize figures of soldiers in armor guarded an equal number of tiny dark alcoves. Anni slipped behind one of the figures and disappeared into the gloom of the alcove. George and Kate, still holding the old Prince's arms, waited for a minute that seemed to be endless. Just in front of them, a Finkel guard was felled by a scrubbing brush flung by a muscular cleaner; a student leaped on another guard from behind and bore him to the ground. Then Anni called, "Come on! Quickly!" An opening could dimly be seen in the back of the alcove. Anni bundled the others through it, then pressed a button to close the opening behind them. The hubbub diminished to a mutter; they were in darkness and peace.

Hesitantly they moved ahead. The old Prince stumbled along as best he could, without question or protest. Anni went first, and George gave the old man what support he could from behind. Kate brought up the rear. In the intermittent light from slit windows they struggled on. Though the passage was a little broader than the one Kate had been in before, it was impossible to hurry. Kate lost all sense of time; it was an endless ordeal. Twice she almost fell, and once she grazed an arm on the stonework.

Some distance along, a passage opened out to the left, but Anni ignored it and led on. Soon afterward there was another opening to the right. And now Anni suddenly whispered, "Stop! Listen!"

Toward them along the side passage came the notes of an early Beatles tune, plucked hesitantly from the strings of a guitar. It was the same tune Kate had heard on her first night in the Castle.

"Friedrich!" Kate and Anni exclaimed together.

Anni scampered away toward the sound. Kate and George stayed behind with the Prince, unwilling to urge him away from the escape route.

"I don't believe," said Prince Ferdinand, making his first remark since they'd collected him from his room, "that the boy will ever master that thing."

The sound of the guitar ceased. Anni's voice was heard, calling to them. And the old Prince himself led the way, shuffling along the side passage.

At the end of the passage a door was open and electric light streamed out. In the doorway stood Dr. Stockhausen.

"My dear Prince!" he said. "Welcome to my refuge. It's the Prime Ministerial fallout shelter. Who's in power at the moment?"

26

◄◀《 》▶►

"My wife and I are perfectly comfortable here," said Dr. Stockhausen a few minutes later. "All *I* wish is that Prince Friedrich would give up practicing on that wretched instrument. If he went on much longer, Karl would confiscate it."

Karl grinned evilly and made a pretended grab at the guitar. Friedrich clutched it to himself.

"I'm d-doing much better than I was," he said.

It turned out that the Stockhausens were installed in a modest but well-equipped apartment with running water and ample stores. During his thirty-year Prime Ministership, Dr. Stockhausen had provided for all eventualities. With Karl as combined manservant, guard, and reconnaissance patrol, the Stockhausens were in a position to bide their time indefinitely.

They declined an invitation to leave Essenheim on board the *Lorelei*. "When we learn from Karl that an acceptable regime has come into being," said Dr. Stockhausen, "we shall emerge. However, if Prince Friedrich should decide to leave now, we would not stand in his way."

207

Kate had the impression that this last remark was an understatement.

Friedrich beamed happily. "I'd love to c-come," he said. "I'll be ready in a m-minute."

Anni was anxious not to lose time. "Hansi and River-man Flusswasser will be waiting for us at the quay," she said. "I don't want anything to go wrong now."

With Friedrich added to the party, and the old Prince a little revived, they returned to the point at which they'd left the main passage. A little farther on, its sides ceased to be cut stone and became jagged rock. There was less height, and they all had to bend low. Occasional trickles of water could be heard. Once again the journey seemed to drag on endlessly, and the old Prince stumbled several times and had to be helped to his feet. And then ahead of them there was dim light, filtering round an obstruction.

"We're coming out on the cliff face," Anni said.

"What's that in the way?"

"It's only a bush. Covers the entrance." Anni pushed her way around it. Kate, George, Friedrich, and the old Prince followed with difficulty. They were in open air, on a narrow path that led round the cliff, with the sheer walls of the castle above. The rain had stopped and there was full moonlight. From far below, loud in the silence, the roar of the Esel River could be heard.

Kate swayed, suddenly dizzy. Anni grabbed her arm.

"Are you all right, Kate?"

"Yes."

Slowly and perilously they edged their way round

the cliff. The old Prince tottered along between George and Kate, holding a hand of each. He looked as if he might fall at any moment and take them with him. Even without the Prince, Kate couldn't have managed this journey in normal times and in the light of day; her head for heights was poor and her limbs would have refused to carry her. But now there was no alternative and she struggled on, too exhausted to be frightened.

It could only have been a few minutes, but once again it felt like hours, before there was the sound of water much closer at hand, and they were coming off the cliff face and into the course of a fast-flowing stream that splashed its way down into the Esel.

"This is where we get wet," said Anni. "It's a good thing it isn't higher."

They waded the broad, shallow stream. Kate gasped at the coldness of the water. Then they were on the far bank, and on rounding another corner were under the supports of the castle bridge, at the town end.

Cautiously they climbed to road level. There were no guards here. Anni took the Prince's arm, relieving Kate, and they made their laborious way along the High Street toward the marketplace. In the square the people were massing. It was an orderly concourse, without much noise. Out of the dark side streets came more and more quiet folk to swell the gathering. A voice could be heard marshaling them through a bullhorn.

"It's the Mayor!" George said. "It worked! They responded to the *Free Press*!"

Kate caught a note of longing in his voice. "We can manage now, George," she said. "Go on. Follow the story."

"Oh, no!" declared George. "We're getting you away first. That's the priority." And Kate didn't argue.

They made their way round the edge of the square and continued toward the quay. It took a long time to pass the gathering host. It seemed as if every man, woman, and child in Essenheim were assembling. Not one had a weapon. And then, in response to a call through the bullhorn, the column moved off. The people of Essenheim were on their way to the castle. In the moon-shadowed streets none of them recognized that their Prince of so many years was passing them in the other direction.

They were in steep deserted streets now, heading downhill toward the quay. The sound of a running diesel engine could be heard. The *Lorelei* was under power and ready to go. As they reached the water's edge, a gangplank was let down. Hansi and Able Riverman Flusswasser waited on the boat with arms outstretched to help them on board. There was a last perilous moment as George pushed the stumbling Prince ahead of him; Riverman Flusswasser leaned far out to grab his hands and pull him on board. Anni, Kate, and Friedrich followed George, and then they were all safe on the rear deck of the *Lorelei*.

Hansi cast off. The quay fell behind and the sloping streets of Essenheim moved past as the riverman steered the launch down the Esel. The lights of the hilly town gleamed high and low. Above them

210

on one side loomed the castle; on the other side, farther away, was the red light at the top of the radio antenna.

"How long will it take us to get to the border?" Kate asked as the boat left Essenheim town and began to throb its way gently between vineyards.

"A couple of hours, maybe," Anni said. "The border posts are at the lock."

"Could we be stopped there?"

"We're not *going* to be!" said Anni with determination. "Then I'll take Uncle Ferdy to my cousin's, where he wants to go. And *then* . . ." Her eyes sparkled. "Then London, here I come! Just think, Kate, I'll be seeing you in London. Can you believe it?"

"Only just," Kate admitted. She could hardly believe anything that had happened in the last couple of weeks. Even this boat trip down the river had taken on an air of unreality. Surely it wasn't actually happening?

Anni and Friedrich went with the old Prince into the *Lorelei's* cabin. Only Kate and George remained on deck. They stood side by side, leaning on the rails. Kate felt a surge of affection for George, and with it another sensation: a slight electric sense of physical nearness. Perhaps after all the presence of George could do something for her. . . .

"Kate," said George softly.

"Yes, George?"

"Kate, may I tell you something? Do you know . . ." George hesitated, then took the plunge. "Kate, you look almost beautiful in the dark!"

Laughter bubbled up in Kate. She didn't feel insulted at all. George's assessment of her charms was roughly

211

the same as her own. Maybe she pleased Essenheimisch taste, but she was leaving Essenheim now.

Then there was a disturbance, the creak of a door. Opening onto the deck at the rear of the cabin was a tall locker where brooms and buckets were kept. The door of the locker now moved. Something inside fell over and there was a muttered curse in Essenheimisch. And then the door was thrown wide, and out of it stepped Rudi.

Kate and George stared. Rudi was disheveled, and much less self-possessed than usual.

"Kate!" he said. "I had to see you again! I hated watching you walk away from me this morning. Kate, believe me, when I said I wanted to marry you, I really meant it. It wasn't merely Herr Finkel's wish. I *do* care for you!"

Kate was silent. Rudi went on, "Truly, Kate. Since we first met, I've cared for you more and more. In Essenheim or out of it, whatever happens, I love you!"

His tone was earnest. Kate looked him in the eye. Suddenly, for the first time, she was sure that he meant exactly what he said. At least, he meant it right now. She could have her Prince if she wanted.

And she was sure, too, for the first time, that she didn't want him. As recently as this morning, she had hesitated. But at last the magic had stopped working. This was the man who'd changed sides three times, who'd proposed to Elsa Schweiner to save his title and afterward ditched her. This was the man who'd behaved so callously to his uncle and who'd tried to win her by blackmail.

212

"Rudi," she said, "I wouldn't want you if you were the last man alive!"

Rudi stared. Obviously he couldn't at first believe what he'd heard. Then his face darkened. "It's because of *this* fellow, isn't it?" he said. "Our friend the scribbler. I should never have let him come with us!"

Unnoticed, George had been opening the section of railings where the gangplank would be lowered when the boat tied up. Now he was facing Rudi.

Unconscious of the gap behind him, Rudi took a step forward. "I don't like you, George," he said. "I don't like you at all."

"That's all right," said George amiably. "You don't have to." And then, "Rudi, can you swim?"

"Of course I can swim!" said Rudi. "Why?"

"Show us," said George, and pushed him overboard. The last they saw of Rudi was his head breaking the surface and his arms moving as he struck out for the bank.

"George!" exclaimed Kate. She was shocked. It was totally unlike George: so drastic, so dramatic. "How could you? *That's* not a reporter's job! What would the *Daily Intelligence* say?"

Then she was in his arms.

27

The *Lorelei* moved gently into the lock at the Serenian border. Ex-Prince Laureate Ferdinand Franz Josef III emerged from the cabin, climbed painfully on deck, and stood at the rails between Kate and Anni. "I must look my last on Essenheim," he said.

At the top end of the lock was a tiny wooden hut with a lamp hanging above the door. Out of the hut stepped a man in the coarse purple uniform of Essenheim officialdom.

"Who's on board?" he called as the boat came to a standstill.

"I am," said the old Prince.

"Why, Highness!" said the man. "It's you! You're leaving all that shambles behind, eh? I don't blame you!" He moved away, grinning, and began to spin a great wheel. Slowly the top gate of the lock closed behind the *Lorelei*.

"When you come out at the bottom end," the lock-keeper said, "you'll be in Serenia. Good-bye, Highness, and good luck. Heaven help Essenheim!" He came to attention and saluted.

Solemnly, shakily, the old Prince returned the salute. "Heaven help Essenheim!" he said.

As the boat began slowly to sink in the lock, somebody leaped perilously ashore, and in a moment had vanished into the darkness—back into Essenheim. The last thing Kate saw as the boat sank down into the cavernous depths of the lock was the lockkeeper's face as he stared openmouthed after the disappearing figure.

"What *is* George doing?" Anni asked in astonishment.

"What do you *think* he's doing?" said Kate. "He's seen us safely to the border. Now he's gone back to follow the story!"

The front gate opened, and the *Lorelei* glided out into Serenia.

28

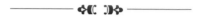

Kate flew into London Airport on an Air Serenia flight a couple of days later. Her father was waiting for her, having taken time out from the office. He said, "Hello."

Kate said, "Hello."

Edward said, "Well, how did it go?"

Kate said, "Oh, not so badly."

Edward said, "There were telephone troubles, weren't there?"

Kate said, "Yes, and revolutions and things. Were you worried?"

Edward said, "Not much. I knew you could look after yourself. And even if you couldn't, I knew George would look after you."

Kate said, "Have you heard from George?"

Edward said, "Yes, he came through on the phone last night. He's got some pretty good stuff. George is a bright lad."

Kate said, "Yes."

Edward said, "Nice, too. I like him."

Kate said, "So do I."

There was a brief silence. Then Edward said, emotionally, "Oh, Kate, I did miss your cooking!"

Kate said, "You are an unreconstructed male chauvinist pig!"

They hugged each other for a long time.

George stayed in Essenheim for another week. He came back and wrote a series of articles in the *Daily Intelligence* under the general heading REVOLUTION IN A NUTSHELL. They attracted a lot of notice, and George won a "Reporter of the Year" award and a hefty pay increase.

George and Kate are still fond of each other. Kate is now at the University of West Yorkshire, studying modern languages and enjoying life. She hasn't made any plans for her future yet. When she does, George hopes to be included in them.

Anni arrived in London after three weeks in Serenia. She spent a month with her friend Betsy, then came to Edward and Kate on a short visit that kept prolonging itself. She is still there, having for all intents and purposes become Edward's daughter and Kate's sister. Hansi is a student at the London School of Printing. He spells better in English than he ever did in Essenheimisch. Hansi and Anni are still starry-eyed about each other.

Ex-Prince Laureate Ferdinand Franz Josef III of Essenheim is still alive, though increasingly frail. He is living with his daughter and Prince Friedrich in Serenia and seems contented enough. His forecast that Friedrich would never master the guitar has yet to be disproved. There is some argument, among those who care about such things, over whether Prince Ferdinand was Essenheim's last Prince Laureate, or whether the brief reign of Prince Rudolf should also go into the record books.

And Essenheim itself? Well, when the great march led by the Mayor arrived at the castle, the soldiers and students and cleaning ladies all poured out to meet it, and the people decided there and then that they'd had enough of revolutions and self-appointed leaders, and that they'd take a vote by ballot to find out what they really wanted to do. The result? The people of Essenheim elected to become part of happy, peaceful Serenia. Serenia was quite willing; it had been expecting Essenheim to join it ever since the end of World War I, but was much too civilized to apply any pressure.

There are some, of course, who regret Essenheim's disappearance as an independent country. One of these is Aleksi. Having recently gone through an American phase and discovered the works of John Greenleaf Whittier, he has written a poem in which he appeals, somewhat prematurely, to the Serenians to shoot if they must his old gray head but spare his country's flag. This is universally agreed to be his masterpiece.

Sonia is also dissatisfied, believing that Serenia is bourgeois, elitist, and degenerate. But Sonia enjoys being dissatisfied and wouldn't know what to do with herself if she had the misfortune to become contented, so there's no need to feel sorry for her.

Rudi didn't come to any harm from his ducking in the Esel River. He is now running for election as Essenheim's representative in the Serenian Senate. He'll

probably win. He may well finish up as Federal Presi
dent of Serenia. Whatever happens to those around
him, Rudi will come out on top.

Girls still think Rudi is wonderful, until they find
he doesn't care about them. Some of them find out
too late, and suffer. Yet there was one girl he did care
about, as much as he was able to care, and that was
Kate. If he'd played his cards less cleverly he might
have won her; who knows? He'll never do so now.

The Essenheim Army has been incorporated into
Serenia's. It no longer includes ex-Colonel Schweiner,
who was court-martialed and dismissed from the service in disgrace. The Army now has smart new uniforms, and its duties are purely ceremonial.

The dungeons of Essenheim Castle stand empty.